Ellen was ⎯⎯⎯⎯⎯⎯ ⎯⎯⎯ Herbert would not want her along as a stepdaughter. And her mother couldn't just abandon her, at least not before she was sixteen.

'When you're sixteen you could marry your tall, dark, handsome stranger,' said Isadora.

Davie blinked. 'Tall, dark—'

'Ask Ellie who's tall and dark.'

'No wonder I don't tell you everything, Isadora McBain!'

'You see, Davie, Ellie has a boyfriend. Surprise, surprise! Isn't she the dark horse? She goes to meet him every day—'

The Gooseberry

Joan Lingard

Beaver Books

A Beaver Book
Published by Arrow Books Limited
62-65 Chandos Place, London WC2N 4NW

An imprint of Century Hutchinson Limited

London Melbourne Sydney Auckland Johannesburg
and agencies throughout the world

First published by Hamish Hamilton 1978
Beaver edition 1982
Reprinted 1984 and 1987

Set in Century Schoolbook

Printed and bound in Great Britain by
Anchor Brendon Limited, Tiptree, Essex

ISBN 0 09 934090 9

ONE

'Come on, Ellie!'

Ellen Rose Ferguson, more commonly known as Ellie – to everyone except her mother, in fact – looked up. She had been leaning on the fence contemplating the Water of Leith, letting her eye run with the mud-brown water as it flowed gently between its banks. Now it rippled freely; now it bubbled over a cluster of stones to send little white flurries frothing around a rotting branch and other pieces of flotsam. An old cigarette packet. A man's boot, discarded perhaps by a tramp in favour of something better. Over the years she had seen many things in the river. It was certainly no mighty waterway, like the Clyde or the Thames, but it was Edinburgh's main river and as such she felt it should be held in respect.

'Come on, Ellie!' Isadora called less patiently now, for her companion was urging her on.

'I'm coming.'

Ellen went to join them.

'I don't know why you have to spend hours staring into that scummy old burn.'

'It's a river, Issie. Your trouble is—'

'I know – I have no soul.'

William tightened his hold on Isadora's hand and gazed into her large violet-blue eyes, clearly feeling that he could see her soul reflected in them and so did not believe her. One of Isadora's boyfriends had said he could drown in those eyes. He had been very romantic, won all the poetry competitions at school, had even had a poem published in *The Scotsman*. His poetic compliments had made Isadora giggle and in

5

the end put her off him; she had felt he was practising his poesy on her, that she was for him merely an object. The reasons that Isadora went off boys were as varied as the boys themselves.

Ellen went ahead now lengthening her stride until Isadora began to protest again.

'Oh, Ellie, please! Wait, for goodness' sake!'

Ellen was tall, and not just for her age, as people used to say to her when she was younger, a remark which suggested perhaps that in time others might catch up and then she would be considered only normal. Few had caught up, and certainly not Isadora who reached as high as her shoulders, and so had legs that were correspondingly shorter. Few in their class at school stood near Ellen in height. She often said she had had the ill luck to strike a year of midgets.

And so they proceeded homeward in fits and starts, their progress by no means straightforward, not flowing steadily like the river in one direction, for some streets and alleyways were preferred over others, each of the two girls having her own likes and dislikes. Ellen must follow the river for as long as she could, Isadora chose routes that passed shop windows where she could linger, coveting ancient moth-eaten Paisley shawls, seedy black crêpe dresses left over from the thirties, peachy-pink pure silk petticoats, feather boas, Japanese fans, strings of beads of jade and amber, bedraggled fur coats, *thé dansant* purses on silver chains. It was her ambition to open a shop selling antiques and secondhand clothes when she left school. Edinburgh was coming down with such shops, Ellen told her, but Isadora remained undeterred. William, as far as was known, had no preference about routes: he simply went.

Finally they arrived in the street where the girls lived. The street was lined on either side by tenements, late Georgian, some of which had gone steadily downhill, some of which had been 'coming up' again in the last few years and sported yellow and blue doors and window boxes. On the pavement kids played hopscotch, careered illegally past on skateboards, stotted balls against walls. The only gardens were the shared back greens at the rear of the buildings but children seldom played there leaving them as the preserve of the women for drying their washing, or for the odd person who had green fingers.

On the corner Isadora and William halted to say their goodbyes whilst Ellen waited leaning against the railings of a basement a few yards further along muttering to herself. The cheek of Isadora MacBain! She complained if Ellen loitered for a few seconds and then kept her hanging around for hours.

A shadow appeared beside hers on the pavement.

'Hi, Ellie! Talking to yourself again?'

She transferred her glowering look to Davie Dunlop, her next-door neighbour. She could look down on the top of his curly brown head too. He had tight springy curls which she liked to pull and watch bouncing back into place again. Under his arm he had a stack of newspapers which he was setting out to deliver.

'It's no wonder I talk to myself. With a friend like Isadora! Come on, Issie!'

'I'm coming. Goodbye, William. See you later.' Their palms disengaged, only the fingers remained in touch, lingeringly.

'Goodbye, Sweet William,' called Ellen. 'I hope I don't see you later.'

Isadora moved a couple of inches away from him.

Davie moved off speedily with his newspapers. He never walked, always ran, on noiseless rubber-soled feet. Ellen sighed, audibly. Isadora was coming slowly, taking one step at a time, backwards.

William waited at the corner until the girls had gone into Ellen's stair. It was one of the ones that had not come up yet, entered by a splintered and faded green door, flanked by two rows of dull brass bells. On the threshold Isadora looked back to wave and then Ellen pulled her inside and let the heavy door fall shut behind them. It was murky inside after the bright spring sunshine out. There was a smell of dust, damp, cat, and bleach. Ellen lived with her mother in the top flat, right: they must climb three flights of steep stone stairs, pulling themselves up by the handrail, with Isadora puffing and sighing as she always did. Just because she lived in a ground floor flat!

Ellen unlocked the door and ushered Isadora in. There was no one at home: Mrs Ferguson worked in a department store from nine till five-thirty daily and Mr Ferguson had died when Ellen was three. He had been a piano player, earned his living that way, on and off, getting work in pubs and clubs, and the rest of the time he spent in the dole queue, or the pub; so said Ellen's mother. Oh there was no denying he'd been a brilliant pianist and was a lot of fun some of the time. But such men made difficult husbands, said Ellen's mother.

The girls went to the kitchen, Ellen made coffee and then they carried it through to her bedroom. Isadora said she mustn't stay long, she had her hair to wash. She was always washing her hair. Ellen didn't know how she could be bothered; once a week was more than enough for her.

Ellen's room was covered with posters: wild flowers, pop stars, old theatre ads, pre-Raphaelite reproductions, maps; but in the middle of the room, against the wall, stood her most prized possession, her father's old upright piano. On top of it were three photographs, all of her father, one taken on the beach, another in the Botanic Garden standing beside the slim beautiful trunk of a Chinese birch tree, the third a close-up showing only his head and shoulders. In all three he was laughing. Ellen went up to the third one now, looked him full in the face and greeted him.

'Hi, Pa!'

Isadora glanced uneasily at her. 'What's the matter?' Ellen demanded. 'Why don't you like me saying hello to my dad when I come in? You say hello to yours, don't you?' That was different, said Isadora. Well, of course it was!

'Don't sit down!' Ellen raised her hand. She had a job for Isadora to do first: Isadora must measure her. Isadora groaned, protesting that she had measured her only a few days ago. It was a full week, declared Ellen, she had marked it in her diary. Isadora put down her coffee and Ellen went to stand against the wall where she had her height chart marked out. At the top was written in red letters, 'SIX FEET: GIANTS START HERE.' One inch below was a mark, a small black line, showing Ellen's height the last time she was measured. One of her biggest dreads was that she would reach six feet.

Isadora pulled a box from under the bed and climbed up on it. Ellen passed her a ruler. Ellen stood firm and straight, staring straight ahead, then Isadora laid the ruler horizontally along the top of her head.

'Well?'

'Five feet eleven.'

'Are you sure?'

'Certain. Cross my heart.'

'You're not lying?'

'Would I?'

'Yes. If you wanted to sweeten me up.'

Isadora climbed down from the stool grumbling that it was some job trying to sweeten Ellen up. But she would come to the school disco tonight with her, wouldn't she? She would give her her enamelled pendant if she did. At that Ellen sat up and took a little notice – she had stretched out on the floor and was watching a shaft of sunlight playing across the ceiling – and asked if Isadora meant the green one. She wavered. She sighed.

'You will come?'

'But I'm sick of playing gooseberry to you and William. Or Gerry. Or Colin.'

'There'll be other boys there, Ellie.'

'All four feet two! So then I can get to be a wall-flower. At least wallflowers look nicer, and smell better.'

Isadora continued wheedling. Ellen had always liked the green pendant, hadn't she? She could have it for keeps, not just on loan. 'Come on, Ellie!' Oh all right! Ellen collapsed. Her trouble, she moaned, was that she had no will power, she could be bought off with a bag of chips.

Now Isadora must fly to wash her long, silky, blonde hair. She would see Ellen at ten to seven and no later! She went, her hair swinging back in a soft fold behind her. Ellen got up from the floor and leant on the mantelpiece, putting both elbows on it and propping her chin between her hands. She stared at herself in the chipped gilt-framed mirror. Her father had brought it home from a pub one night, *en lieu* of payment. There was nothing silky about her hair: it was thick and coarse like a pot scourer and the colour of burnt carrots. She had her father's hair and her father's eyes (chestnut brown) and her father's build. Her mother was *petite* – no other word would do – and her name was Rose which suited her. Ellen sighed.

She abandoned her image and went to the piano.

'Who cares about silky hair? Not you nor me, Pa! Isn't that right? We care about other things.'

She began to play, idly, picking out a few bars, humming as she did, words gradually forming in her head. 'They call me the gooseberry, 'cos I'm always alone. . . . Walking one on the outside. . . . With the other two in.' Suddenly she crashed her hands down on the keys. 'Quit feeling sorry for yourself!' she said aloud, then looked up at her father's smiling face and grinned. 'Doesn't get you anywhere, does it? You never did feel sorry for yourself. No, I know you

10

didn't.' Now she played fluently, a piece of jazz that had been one of his favourites. She played by ear for her mother would not let her have piano lessons. Mrs Ferguson hated the piano; she spoke of it as if it were some nasty dark monster with primeval powers. It brought back bad memories, Ellen supposed; she had long since ceased to argue and took 'cello lessons, as her mother wished, and played the piano for her own amusement. No, it was more than that! The piano was one of the most important things in her life.

She was eating beans and toast in the kitchen when her mother came in from work, puffing and sighing. She was carrying a carton of groceries; she was tired, as usual, and her feet were killing her for it had been hot in the shop and she had had to help out on the children's floor which was not as peaceful as the cosmetics. She kicked off her shoes and wished she didn't have to work. She had two dreams: one was to be able to stop working, at least full-time, so that she could get a bit of time to herself, and the other was to live in a nice wee bungalow in a nice quiet suburb in a nice quiet street and get away from this dreich, cat-smelling stair and dirty, noisy street. The first of her mother's dreams Ellen did not mind, and indeed had decided that when she started to work herself then she could help make it come true. The second she did not take seriously since there was little chance that they could ever afford it. It was all part of the talk of when their ship came in and they'd have a car and shop at Jenners (on account naturally) and go to the Seychelles or Tobago for their holidays. The kitchen drawer was stuffed full of travel leaflets. The furthest they had got so far had been the English Lake District on a five-day coach tour. Ellen had sprained her ankle getting out of the bus at Windermere (it wasn't as though her injury had the nobility of being suffered on a mountain top), and it rained ceaselessly from morning till night, though the nights had been dry and starry. Her mother was now taking a drink of cold water to cool herself down.

'Want some beans, Mum?'

There were a few left glued to the bottom of the pot. But Ellen should have known her mother never ate beans since they were fattening and, anyway, her mother was going out for a meal. Ellen didn't mind, did she? Ellen shook her head and got up to scrape out the pot. Her mother went out quite often in the evenings, usually for a drink. After working hard all day she needed to get some enjoyment out of life: Ellen had often heard her say so to her friend, Mavis. She had a number of women friends with whom she sat in hotel lounges sipping vodka and orange and sometimes they came to the flat and drank cheap wine and Ellen carried in sandwiches. 'My, what a big girl you're getting, Ellen! Isn't she, Rose?' They didn't mean anything by their comments, her mother always said afterwards. And no one could deny that Ellen was big, least of all herself. As she sat demolishing the last of the dried up beans and watching her mother move lightly around the kitchen putting away the groceries, she made yet another resolution to try to improve herself. Isadora, who did not need to improve herself, said it was possible, if one worked at it consistently.

'I think I'll go on a diet,' said Ellen.

'Good idea. No more beans or buns or chips!'

Ellen felt depressed just to hear the words uttered. The worst aspect of dieting was trying to pass the chip shop. The smell drew her like honey draws bees. Her mother was forever complaining that her hair reeked of frying.

Mrs Ferguson went off to get changed, Ellen made herself another piece of toast deciding she required extra fuel to help cope with the disco. She regretted now saying she would go, pendant or no pendant. Her mother returned needing to be zipped up the back and to have her hair admired. She squinted into the little mirror on the dresser and made up her eyes carefully and patiently. What a fuss to go and meet the 'girls' as she called them! Ellen didn't ask where exactly she was going. They asked few questions of one another, unlike Isadora's mother who cross-examined Isadora every time she went across the doorstep. Ellen volunteered that she was going to the school disco and Mrs Ferguson said that that was nice, have a good time, and come home with Isadora. She patted up the back of her hair, stepped away from the mirror to survey the finished effect and then turned to Ellen to ask how she looked. Ellen shrugged, said she looked OK. Only that? No, great. Lovely. Was she sure? Yes, she was sure. What was all the fuss about? Her mother did not usually care about her opinion.

At last Mrs Ferguson was gone, leaving a trail of flowery perfume hanging in the air to mingle with the smell of baked beans and singed toast.

As Ellen was letting herself out to go and meet Isadora she bumped into Davie on the landing. He lived in the top flat left.

'You're not going out, are you, Ellie? I was going to ask you to help me with my physics.'

'And I'd been going to ask you to help me with my French.' Ellen explained how Isadora had bribed her to go to the disco and how her spirit might be strong but her flesh was most definitely weak, to which Davie nodded and said amen. They sat down side by side on the top step and Davie pulled out a bag of black and white striped boilings, one of Ellen's favourite sweets.

'I'm supposed to be on a diet,' she said, her cheek bulging over the hard round sweet.

Davie snorted, unimpressed by such pronouncements, knowing Ellen as he did, and having known her for most of her fourteen years. The Dunlops had moved into their flat when Davie and Ellen were both four years old. He observed that Isadora twisted Ellen round her little finger. Had he noticed the size of Isadora's little finger and had he seen the size of her? asked Ellen. They laughed and Ellen stretched her legs out so that they reached two steps down. She would much rather have helped Davie with his physics and eaten striped boilings than have to go and hang about the school hall having her ears deafened and pretend that she was having a good time. Next time she would resist, she resolved. Davie said he would believe it when he saw it.

They heard the downstairs' door opening and then thudding shut, followed by quick light steps. A whistle from below, made by sticking two fingers in the sides of the mouth, and a voice called, 'Ellie! Are you there, Ellie?'

'I am here, Isadora MacBain!' Ellen hollered down through cupped hands.

It was clear that Isadora was impatient to be off. Various noises travelling upward suggested that she was. If her mother could only hear her! She had such plans for her daughter, wanted her to be artistic in some form or other. And Isadora could hardly draw for toffee! Had Mrs MacBain given up on the idea of her being a ballet dancer? asked Davie, reminiscing on the Saturday mornings when the two girls were dispatched to dancing school where neither of them could dance. 'You're all legs, Ellen,' the teacher used to shriek.

'Ellie!' Isadora's thin thread of patience was about to snap. William would be waiting anxiously on the corner.

'OK, keep your hair on! I'm coming. See you, Davie.'

'Have a good time,' said Davie gloomily.

Ellen bounded off down the stairs, Davie remained on the top step staring morosely into space.

The disco turned out to be everything that Ellen had expected. She spent half the time sitting in the cloakroom reading a book that she had prudently brought with her: *The Last Tycoon* by Scott Fitzgerald. As she read she longed for glamour, men in evening jackets to idolise her, and six inches off her height. The cloakroom smelt of cigarette smoke and old gym shoes and one girl kept being sick at intervals into a basin. Ellen read doggedly on ignoring everything and everybody around her until Isadora arrived, refusing to be ignored. She had come to do a bit of bullying and let off some steam. Elen was so infuriating: she never gave herself a chance, scowled if anyone of the opposite sex came near her, yawned repeatedly, and didn't even get up to dance with other girls. She didn't like dancing with girls, said Ellen; besides she only wanted peace and quiet. She hated being in a situation where you had to be selected. It was all right when teams were being picked for races or tugs of war for then she was in prime demand. But when it came to sex appeal she did not appear to have what it took. One had to face up to the facts of life.

'Oh shut up! You make me sick.' Isadora glanced at the girl bent over the basin and wrinkled her nose.

She insisted on dragging Ellen back to the hall. One of the male teachers danced with her; he came up to her shoulder and she trod on his toes whenever they closed in on one another. After that she sat along the wall and read her book, with her fingers in her ears. So she played her part of wallflower.

Following directly on from that she became a gooseberry again. At least she was versatile, she thought, as she scuffed her way along the pavement behind Isadora and William, although the two roles were of course exceedingly compatible. They stopped off at Sam's café for another session of noise and smoke. Stomach awash with coke, head spinning with sound, eyes strained from trying not to look at her two companions who had eyes only for one another, Ellen considered how incredible it was that this was what some people called an 'evening out'.

Her mother was always going on about evenings out telling her that she should have more of them and not spend so much time hanging around the flat. Hanging around playing the piano. She longed to be doing just that right now. She sat up and caught Isadora's eye.

'Just another five minutes, Ellie.'

'Have another coke,' said William.

'No thanks.'

'Pendant really suits you, Ellie.'

'Flattery will get you nowhere, Isadora.'

'There's Davie,' said William, diverting a potential argument.

Davie had come into the café and was buying a bottle of lemonade at the counter. His mother drank lemonade and ate ginger nuts every evening whilst she watched the television. Clutching the bottle to his chest he came over to speak to them. Come and sit down, said William, but Davie was on his way to the chip shop. His Uncle Harry had been in, he'd had a win on the dogs and given him a pound. He looked at Ellen. If she liked he'd buy her a spring roll and chips. Ellen was up at once.

'Mention chips to Ellie and there's no holding her,' said Isadora. 'Like one of those game dogs on the scent.'

'Whilst you, Issie, just exist on love. Anyway, I'm sure Sweet William will see you home safely and if I meet your dad I'll tell him the big bad wolf got you.'

Ellen felt better the minute the first chip passed her lips. And the spring roll was hot and delicious and squishy inside. They ambled homeward munching and Ellen told Davie how awful the disco had been. He said that just reinforced his own opinion of such forms of entertainment; he would rather play football. 'Me too,' said Ellen fervently.

It was bucket night in the street: the dustbins were out, and the cardboard boxes and the plastic bags lined the pavements awaiting collection in the morning. The street was disgusting after bucket nights, said Ellen's mother: another reason that she wanted the bungalow in the quiet street. In such streets people did not have that kind of rubbish. They passed an old man bent over a bin. A bucket-raker. Ellen had sometimes considered the idea of bucket-raking; apparently it was astonishing what folk did throw out at times. But her mother would have a pink canary if she saw her and, apart from that consideration, the thought of the muck she would have to rake amongst did rather put her off.

Davie deposited his chip paper in the bucket marked *Morrison* in squint black painted letters. It belonged to Granny Morrison who lived on their stair and had a voice like a corncrake which she liked to vent from her window. She and Ellen's mother had not spoken since they had had a tiff over washing the stair some five years back. That was yet another reason why Mrs Ferguson wanted the nice wee bungalow.

Ellen was still eating: she liked to make her chips last, to prolong her pleasure.

'Didn't realise I was so hungry. My mum says I've got hollow legs.' She looked down. ''Course there's a lot of them to fill.'

'My mum says she doesn't know where all my food goes to. Not to my height anyway.' He sounded mournful.

'I was thinking, Davie, maybe you should try stretching exercises. Hanging from the top of the door and things like that.'

'I could always get put on the rack.'

'Well, it must be easier to stretch than to shrink. There's hope for you but none for me.'

Without enthusiasm he said he supposed so. They had better go in now as his mother would be wondering where he'd got to.

They climbed the stairs and as they passed Granny Morrison's door on the second landing Ellen made a feint towards the bell pretending she was going to pull it.

'Don't, Ellie! She'd eat the head off you.'

'I'm not scared of auld Granny Morrison. Besides, she can't reach my head.'

Davie's mother was waiting at the top of the stairs for her lemonade.

'You've been an awful long time, Davie. I'm fair dying of thirst. Oh hello, Ellie. Your mum's home. I think you've got a visitor.'

She would have been looking through her spy-hole. Davie's father had put it in the door because his wife was supposed to be nervous about burglars and wanted to make sure she was not going to open the door to one but Mrs Ferguson maintained that Mrs Dunlop had had it put in so that nothing would go past her. The Fergusons had to pass the Dunlops' door to get to their own.

The visitor would doubtless be Mavis or Netta or Olive and the two women would be having a confidential wee chat on the settee that would break off in mid-sentence when Ellen opened the door.

'See you in the morning, Ellie,' said Davie. 'I'll ring your bell.'

Ellen said good-night to Davie and his mother and went along the landing to her own door. She had polished up their brass nameplate the day before. It shone on the dim landing. *Ferguson*, it said. She liked polishing up the plate, did it with loving care, as Davie had said whilst he sat on the step watching her.

She unlocked the door, stepped into the hall.

'Is that you, Ellen Rose?' called her mother in the tinkly voice that she adopted after drinking a couple of vodkas and orange. 'I'm in the sitting room.'

Ellen opened the sitting-room door, chip bag in hand. She stopped on the threshold. Sitting on the settee beside her mother, obviously having broken off in the middle of a confidential wee chat, was a man in a navy-blue suit.

TWO

Mrs Ferguson checked the flood of irritation that swelled up in her as she regarded her daughter standing in the doorway clutching a grease-stained brown paper in one hand and a chip in the other. The chip was poised half-way to her half-open mouth. She stood as if riveted to the spot, staring at the man. She wore the usual aged jeans which had been patched and repatched, each time with a different colour of material and thread, exceedingly grubby gym shoes with one grey lace undone, and a collarless man's shirt bought at a jumble sale. Ellen and Isadora would travel miles to jumble sales on Saturday afternoons, much to the displeasure of their mothers. Mrs Ferguson knew that she should not bother about her daughter's clothes and it annoyed her that she did. To crown the picture, Ellen's hair stood out about her head like a burning bush. For the umpteenth time her mother resolved that she simply must get her inside a hairdresser's.

'Ellen, dear, come and meet Herbert.'

Herbert stood up, clearing his throat. He might come up to her chin, Ellen estimated, certainly no further. It seemed to be where most people she encountered stopped.

She trailed into the room, the loose lace flapping. As she approached the settee, she all but tripped on it; she did a sideways slide, staggered, clutched at the settee arm for support and lost the rest of her chips from the paper. With a wail she dropped to her knees to rescue them. Mrs Ferguson stared down helplessly at the top of her daughter's head.

'Can I help?' asked Herbert, clearing his throat one more time.

'No, no, Herbert. You don't want to get all greasy.'

Ellen had re-gathered the chips into the paper and was sitting back on her haunches to survey them. They were truly a sorry looking sight. 'Put the blessed thing into the fireplace for a minute!' said Mrs Ferguson, losing some of her smiling calm. As Ellen did as she was told, her mother sent her an eye signal before looking back to Herbert and giving him a little shrug which as much as said: 'These young ones!' They must be tolerant. It would all pass, in time.

'Now then, Ellen, this is Herbert Hall, a very good friend of mine. Herbert, this is my daughter, Ellen Rose.' The introduction was made with a hint of gaiety. Or desperation perhaps?

Ellen extended a hand, as did Herbert. His wavered first and then she withdrew hers to wipe it on the back of her jeans. It was not what her mother would call presentable.

'Never mind the hand shaking,' cried Mrs Ferguson. 'Let's take it as read. Sit down, dear, and tell us all about the disco.'

'It was lousy.'

Ellen sat down on an upright chair some distance away from the settee. From there she could look through their own uncurtained window to the windows on the other side of the street. Several were also uncurtained allowing her to see lit rooms and people inside them, some moving about, some sitting in front of television sets. One man in a string vest was shaving with an open razor in front of his window. He did it every evening. An exhibitionist, said her mother.

'That was too bad,' said Herbert.

'Oh, they're always lousy.'

'We had a lovely meal,' said Mrs Ferguson. 'Really lovely.' She smiled at Herbert.

Herbert looked at Ellen and then back at her mother. 'She's not very like you, is she, Rose?'

20

'I'm like my dad.'

'Oh yes. Yes, of course.'

'Spitting image everyone says. He was six feet three in his stockinged feet.'

'Good height that.'

'Built to match too. Really broad shoulders he had.'

'Was it raining when you came in, dear? I thought it might turn to rain, didn't you, Herbert?'

'He played rugby. Scrum half. If he'd lived he might have been capped for Scotland.'

'Now, Ellen, I don't think he was *that* good.'

'He was. Everyone says so. Did you ever play rugby, Mr Hall?'

Herbert was not able to say that he had. He confessed that he was not really the sporty type, though he had played badminton. So had she, Mrs Ferguson jumped in eagerly, and for a few seconds they rediscovered the joys of badminton in church halls, whilst Ellen picked a bit of the sole of her gym shoe. After that they had silence broken by Herbert commenting that Ellen seemed very fond of chips? She affirmed that she was. Her dad had been too. He used to have a black pudding supper every Saturday night after he'd been playing.

'He played the piano, didn't he?' Herbert's throat was giving him a lot of bother. His Adam's apple gulped up and down and a blush of red tinged his narrow cheekbones.

'He was a brilliant pianist. Absolutely fabulous. He could have been a proper concert pianist if he'd wanted, played in the Usher Hall—'

'That's enough now, dear,' said Mrs Ferguson gently. 'I must warn you, Herbert, that Ellen does tend to embroider a teeny bit.'

'Mum thinks I don't remember just because I was only three when Dad died. But I do remember! I remember everything.'

Herbert glanced again from one to the other and blinked. He said that he believed that some people did have total recall. The writer Compton Mackenzie had claimed he could remember being pushed in his pram. That was like her! declared Ellen. Mrs Ferguson said she was being silly. Herbert looked down at the bumps of his knees.

'Do you play the piano, Mr Hall?' asked Ellen.

'Herbert's in Insurance,' said Mrs Ferguson.

Herbert apologised, saying that wasn't very exciting but this Mrs Ferguson disputed. She thought it would be fascinating. Ellen observed that she didn't think her father would have been much interested in insurance and her mother said tartly that it might have been better for them if he had been.

A noise down in the street prevented any further discussion on the joys of insurance. Mr Burns was coming home. He lived in the basement of the next stair, a meek and mild little man except when he went to the pub and then he underwent a character change, becoming garrulous and aggressive with it. He liked then to let the world know what he thought of it and would stand on the pavement, before disappearing underground, and utter his reproach well salted with curses, fists raised heavenward in an angry clench. He was another reason why Mrs Ferguson fancied a bungalow.

Mrs Ferguson jumped up and said it was time she got some supper and would Ellen like to come and help her? Herbert seemed bewitched by the voice in the street. The invective was especially rich with four-lettered words tonight. Ellen giggled. Mrs Ferguson switched on the television, flicking through the three channels in rapid succession and coming to rest on an old film. That looked safe. Herbert could watch whilst they got the supper.

'Come on, Ellen! And bring your chip paper.'

'I'm coming.' Ellen did not move.

Mrs Ferguson left, with another meaningful look. She had a whole range of looks by which she communicated with Ellen.

'This is a nice big room,' said Herbert, who seemed to feel he should say something. He craned his neck to examine the plaster cornice and the central ceiling rose. 'Nice high ceiling.'

Ellen nodded. What kind of room did he live in? she wondered. And with whom? Best not to ask.

'*Ellen!*'

'I'm coming.'

This time she went, taking the offensive chip paper with her.

Her mother was busy in the kitchen making coffee (real, not instant), setting a tray with a lace cloth and her best china, cutting up a quiche and laying out sandwiches on a silver salver covered with a doily. Ellen stared. What was it all for? Their supper of course, what else? Mrs Ferguson had purchased the quiche and sandwiches already made before coming home. She moved briskly about the kitchen; Ellen leant against the table pinching a crumb off the tart and opening up the sandwiches to see what was inside. They didn't usually eat all that before they went to bed. Wasn't it supposed to be bad for you, not to say fattening, to eat so much before sleeping? She had always been told that it was. She was to go and wash her hands and smarten herself up a bit, ordered her mother. She was like a tink. Honestly!

'Racial discrimination,' said Ellen, extracting a slice of onion.

'Don't, Ellen! And go and—'

Yes, yes, she was going. She departed to her bedroom with the lace of her shoe slapping the hall floor making little clicking sounds which she quite enjoyed. She closed the door, went to the piano and sat down. She looked up at her father.

'Badminton, I ask you! And he'll be lucky if he's five feet two . . . with his boots on!'

Her father smiled back, understanding everything.

She sighed, began to pick out a few notes on the keyboard.

'They call me the gooseberry
Always sitting alone
Whilst the other two . . . whisper
And want to be on their own.'

She started as the door opened behind her. Her mother, shaking her head, advanced into the room. What was she playing the piano for now? They were waiting for her to come and join them. Did she have to? She wasn't hungry and would rather stay where she was.

'I want you to come, dear.'

'I don't ask you to sit with Isadora and me.'

'That's different.'

'How is it?'

'You know it is.'

Ellen played a couple of notes.

'Leave that damned thing alone! I wish I'd burnt it when—'

'You wouldn't dare? You wouldn't?' Ellen's eyes, so like her father's, dilated with horror.

Mrs Ferguson subsided. She sighed. No, of course she wouldn't, she hadn't really meant it, it was just that Ellen was so exasperating at times!

'Please, love, come through, for my sake.'

'But, Mum, he's your friend. He's got nothing to do with me, has he?'

'I don't know, Ellen. But he might well have.'

Mrs Ferguson turned and left the room.

Ellen followed.

The supper party was not what Mrs Ferguson would have called a great success. Usually when she had visitors she liked to sum the evening up afterwards, classify it under various headings, such as lively, a bit slow, and so forth. This evening would require an epithet all of its own. To begin with Herbert did not drink coffee after nine o'clock in the evening as it kept him awake. Mrs Ferguson paused, coffee pot suspended over his designated cup, and tried to cope with this unexpected rejection. Visitors were usually thrilled to get real coffee, and this was no cheap stuff either mixed with chicory. Ellen quickly offered to make Herbert a cup of cocoa but he did not want anyone to be troubled on his behalf; half a cup of cold milk would do him nicely.

'Cold milk,' echoed Mrs Ferguson bleakly.

Ellen poured it.

'A piece of quiche, Herbert?'

He hesitated.

'It's cheese and onion.'

Oh. Did cheese keep him awake too? asked Ellen. Not exactly, but it did make him dream. What was wrong with that? Ellen was astonished by the idea that anyone might dislike dreaming.

'Please don't eat it if you don't want to, Herbert. Ellen, pass Herbert the salami sandwiches.'

'Salami,' stammered Herbert.

Ellen lifted the plate with a flourish — she was beginning to enjoy herself — and as she swooped it in a wide arc towards Herbert she lost a sandwich. In a flash she had retrieved it and was dusting it off.

'Ellen!' her mother reproved her. 'You know not to. . . .'

The sandwich was laid aside, the others offered. Herbert looked uneasily upon them.

'Salami on rye,' said Ellen. 'Delicious. Or does it make you dream too?' Herbert said that he did not know. 'We'll do an experiment then, shall we?' cried Ellen, refusing to meet her mother's glance which she knew was intended to quell most thoroughly.

'Don't you like salami, Herbert? If so, please don't eat it if you don't want to.'

He admitted that he was rather a plain eater.

'My dad used to eat salami by the yard.'

'Pass Herbert the shortbread then, Ellen. You do like shortbread?'

Indeed he did. Mrs Ferguson settled back with a little sigh of relief. Herbert confessed that he was rather partial to sweet things, and added that his

mother had baked a very good shortbread. His teeth
grazed the edges of the solid looking slab of shortcake
he had taken from the plate. Bought that morning, it
had the aspect of having been left over from New
Year, three years back. Mrs Ferguson inquired if Mrs
Hall had baked a lot.

'Oh yes. She turned out a very light sponge cake, I
must say.' He sighed. 'Very light.'

'Herbert's mother died six months ago, Ellen.'

Through a thick wedge of quiche Ellen said that
she was sorry. The tart was good and in spite of the
spring roll and chips she had discovered she was
hungry. Herbert decided to give his shortbread a rest
but drank up his milk. It appeared that he had lived
with his mother until her death six months ago, his
father having died many years back. He and Mrs
Ferguson exchanged murmurings about loneliness
and missing people and Ellen ate, stretching out for
one piece of quiche after another until her mother
removed the plate from her reach. She transferred
her interest to the salami sandwiches. From time to
time Herbert stole an amazed look at her.

The doorbell rang, startling Mrs Ferguson who wondered who it could be at this time. The only way to find
out was to go and see, said Ellen, preparing to do so but
her mother said that she would go, one never knew.

'It might be someone up to no good,' explained
Ellen after her mother had gone out. She took
another sandwich and Herbert commented that she
seemed to be fond of salami. He and his mother had
never gone much for continental foods; she had been a
good plain cook.

'Mince and potatoes, Scotch broth, that kind of
thing?'

He nodded.

'We like lasagne and spaghetti and hot, hot curries.
The hotter the better.'

Mrs Ferguson returned. It had been Isadora's
father at the door looking for Isadora.

26

'Silly Issie,' said Ellen. 'She'll cop it now. She's got no sense of proportion.'

'Who has?' demanded Mrs Ferguson, before shifting her attention back to her guest. 'More milk, Herbert?'

But Herbert wanted nothing more. He had done very well, thank you.

'Herbert lives in a bungalow on the south side, Ellen,' said her mother.

Ellen's appetite suddenly abandoned her. She laid down the remains of the salami sandwich. 'A bungalow?' she said slowly. 'On the south side?'

It wasn't very big, said Herbert, but he had to confess he was quite fond of it. He liked confessing to things, thought Ellen dully. The garden was rather nice, he went on, and at this time of year the roses were making a really fine show. Mrs Ferguson enthused over that telling him roses were her favourite flowers. Well, they would be, wouldn't they, considering? he said. They smiled at one another, again. Ellen thought she was going to be sick. 'Maybe you and Ellen would like to come to tea on Sunday? Then you could see my little house and garden, that's if you'd like to.'

Oh, they would like to, cried Mrs Ferguson, very much indeed. Wouldn't they, Ellen?

Ellen shook her head sharply in an effort to clear the daze that seemed to have thickened inside it. Her mother and Herbert were beginning to make arrangements, to say four o'clock, that's fine by me. . . . It was certainly not fine by her!

'I'm going to Isadora's for tea on Sunday, Mum.'

'Don't be silly, Ellen. To Isadora's! That doesn't count.' She would not listen to Ellen's protestations about having made promises and said that Isadora and her mother would understand. She would have a word with Mrs MacBain herself.

'You don't need to,' muttered Ellen.

Herbert rose, dusting a few shortbread crumbs

from his knees. He must be going or he would never get up in the morning for his work. Nor would Rose either, eh?

'I hope the shortbread doesn't give you nightmares,' said Ellen.

Herbert's smile looked to her a little queasy.

She turned her back on them and went to the window. Most of the lights had gone out across the street though she could hear music coming from somewhere. Maybe someone was having a party. There was usually some kind of noise going on most of the night. It was that kind of street. They had students and Poles and Pakistanis living in it as well as the more regular-type Edinburgh citizens. Another reason why her mother fancied a bungalow. A bungalow! Never! Ellen turned to see her mother and Herbert standing in the middle of the room smiling at one another in the same goofy way that Isadora and William did.

'See you and Ellen on Sunday then, Rose? I'll look forward to that.'

'So will we, Herbert. Oh, and Ellen, don't forget the bucket!'

Ellen skirted around them and went through the hall into the kitchen. They kept their dustbin in the cupboard there. It was stuffed to overflowing, as usual. She pushed down the rubbish with her foot and then crammed on the lid.

Herbert and her mother were saying good-night at the door. Ellen struggled towards them with the bucket and they had to part to allow her through. Herbert offered help but Mrs Ferguson rejected it out of hand on Ellen's behalf. He could not afford to get his good suit messed up. Besides, Ellen was strong and could easily handle the bucket alone.

They said good-night one more time but did not kiss as Ellen feared they looked about to do. Herbert backed away along the landing nodding and saying, 'See you Sunday, then', and Mrs Ferguson remained

28

in the doorway smiling that secret smile that had been hovering on her lips all evening. As Ellen passed the Dunlops' door she made a face at the spyhole, just in case Davie was peeping. He liked to know what was going on just as much as his mother did.

They began to descend the stairs. Herbert had a bit of trouble with the shadows cast by the railings and once or twice almost missed his footing. Half-way down the first flight a slew of potato peeling escaped from the bucket and Herbert, unsuspectingly arriving on that particular step, slipped. But there was no harm done, he assured Mrs Ferguson, who was hanging over the banister above and had gasped on seeing his head go bobbing downward suddenly. Of course Herbert was not used to stairs, having been born and bred in a bungalow.

Ellen took the bucket down another few steps on to the next landing. She rested against Granny Morrison's door.

'Try not to make so much noise, Ellen,' her mother called down in a loud whisper. 'It's late.'

Herbert caught up with Ellen. They prepared to tackle the next flight.

'My dad used to tear up and down these stairs four and five at a time.'

'Is that a fact?'

'Mum used to say he'd break his leg one of these days. 'Course he never did. . . .'

Ellen was so busy talking and looking behind her at Herbert that she now missed her footing on a worn step, lost balance slightly and then tripped over the dangling shoe lace. She lost hold of the bucket. The lid shot off and the bucket went flying down the entire flight of stairs rolling and bumping and clattering on each one in turn and spilling its contents as it went.

'What's happened?' shouted Mrs Ferguson. 'What's going on?'

Ellen covered her face with her hands. Herbert

remained on the step he had reached clutching the banister rail.

Ellen took her hands away. The mess was prodigious. Tins, peelings, egg shells, tea leaves, greasy papers – including the chip bag – squashed packets, bottles, all the rubbish of the day, littered the stairs. Her shoulders shook; she began to laugh. She laughed and laughed and laughed.

'Ellen, what have you done?'

'I've dropped the bucket.' She felt weak from laughing. She felt she might topple down the stairs herself next to lie amongst the rubbish.

'*Oh no!*'

Doors were opening all up and down the stair. Voices buzzed. Now Davie's was heard.

'What's up? Somebody fallen down the stairs?

'It's Ellen.' Her mother's voice sounded weak and far away. 'She's dropped the bucket.'

'Hang on, Ellie, I'm coming!'

She looked up to see Davie's body come flying down the stairs above her. Faces hung over the banister, Mrs Ferguson's and Mr and Mrs Dunlop's from the top, Mr Mellon's from the second floor; and from the first landing the Smiths and Chisholms peered upward. There were gasps of horror as the spilled rubbish was made out in the gloom. When Davie arrived panting on the landing, Ellen was still laughing.

Then Granny Morrison's door opened and out she came in a grey quilted dressing gown, her grey hair wound into old-fashioned steel curlers that clung grimly to her skull. She laid one broad hand on the banister rail and looked down.

'Is that you, Ellie Ferguson?' she demanded. 'I might have known!'

THREE

The next day Isadora broke up with William and took up with George, and Ellen met Nicolas for the first time. Ellen heard all about William and George but Isadora learned nothing about Nicolas for Ellen had decided that it was time she had a private life.

She met Nicolas through the local minister, the Rev. Augustus Small, whom she encountered in the queue at the greengrocer's and who asked her if she would be interested in giving a helping hand to somebody who needed one. 'You are such a strong sensible girl, Ellen,' said the Rev. Small who was long and thin and stood eye to eye with Ellen. They shuffled along a bit and the minister, clutching a dark green marrow against his chest, told her a little about the person in need. Nicolas was Czechoslovakian and had come over to this country after the war; he was semi-blind with cataracts and was waiting for them to cross his eyes completely before he could have them operated on. He was over seventy and lived alone.

'Poor thing,' said Ellen.

The Rev. Small had known she would be sympathetic and so by the time he had concluded the purchase of his marrow plus a quarter of a pound of monkey nuts he had engaged her as Nicolas's helper.

Nicolas lived five minutes' walk from Ellen's street. His street was what Mrs Ferguson would call 'classier' than theirs, being earlier Georgian, wider, and more elegant. It was also less spotted with rubbish. Presumably its inhabitants had classier buckets, with lids that fitted, and were less partial to carrier bags and cardboard boxes which

31

offered their contents to the winds that savaged the city.

In the flat below Nicolas lived Mavis, one of her mother's cocktail bar friends. As Ellen reached her door Mavis opened it and came out with an empty milk bottle. She smelled of 'Lily of the Valley'; she always did. Ellen was able to identify the perfume because her mother gave Mavis a bottle every Christmas. Mavis knew Nicolas and was delighted that Ellen was going to help him. He was a real pet, she said. She put the snib up on the door and took Ellen up to be introduced.

But before they went inside she nudged her in the ribs and said, 'Hey, I believe you met Herbert yesterday. What did you think of him?'

Ellen shrugged.

'Your mother's not getting any younger, you know, Ellen.'

'Nor am I.'

'Exactly.'

They went inside. Mavis had a key so she did not have to ring the bell and get Nicolas up from his seat. They found him in his high-ceilinged sitting room by one of the two long windows where the sun could touch his face. It was a finely drawn face with high cheekbones, lined but not aged, in a curious way. Ellen liked the look of him at once.

He came to meet them smiling, holding out both hands. It was so good of Ellen to come to his aid, he was immensely grateful.

'Oh, it's nothing.' Ellen took his long slender hand in hers. He was tall too, even taller than she. How she loved people whom she could look up to!

When they sat down she snatched a quick look at the room, getting an impression of plants and paintings and books. And music! For there against the side wall stood a grand piano. It was only because Nicolas's face had been so immediately arresting that she could have missed it. She jumped up exclaiming.

'You like my piano?'

She went to stroke it. The wood gleamed, a deep rich mahogany. She allowed her fingers to slide down to the keys but as soon as a sound escaped she stepped backward. She considered it bad mannered to touch someone else's piano without being invited.

'Please!'

She shook her head. She did not really play properly, only by ear.

Nicolas was a marvellous pianist, said Mavis, he had studied at the conservatoire in Paris and goodness knows where else.

'Music has been my life,' he said with a smile. 'I will play for you later, if you like.'

'Would you?'

He promised.

Mavis said she would leave them to it as her door was ajar and you never knew who was about these days, did you? And apart from that she had a cake in the oven, a piece of which would be brought to Nicolas in due course.

'She is very kind,' said Nicolas after she had gone. 'Everyone is. I am a fortunate man.'

Ellen felt suddenly shy at being left alone with this unknown, talented old man. He began to talk about payment for her services but she said that she had come to do it for nothing. Truly!

'Well, we shall see.'

They agreed that she would come along around five each day and cook his evening meal, clear up and do any chores that he could not cope with. At lunchtime he got 'Meals on Wheels', or else had a sandwich.

'So your name is Ellen,' he mused. 'I like that.'

Ellen Rose Ferguson in full, she informed him, Rose after her mother. He wanted to know if her mother looked like one.

'A bit, yes. She's petite and she always smells nice.'

'She sounds charming.'

'Whereas I'm huge—'

He laughed and she said defiantly, 'But I am. You can't see—,' She broke off embarrassed.

But he could see her outline, he was not totally blind. Her outline was more than enough, she retaliated, making him laugh again. He liked tall girls and no, he was not saying that just to please her! She softened, letting herself smile. She went on to tell him about her friend Isadora and how attractive she was and how the boys flocked around her.

'You must bring her to meet me one of these days.'

That was the last thing she would do, she decided.

Now she told him about her father and his piano playing and how she missed him still, even after all these years. Eleven years. Did it seem silly to Nicolas that she should? He shook his head. He was so easy to talk to, he understood everything she said to him. And he told her a little about his life, how he came from Prague to London with his wife, for he had been married then, and when she had died ten years later he had moved to Edinburgh where he had remained ever since. He liked living here, found it *sympathique*. He still had some family in Czechoslovakia and Paris but had had no children of his own.

'And now, would you like me to play for you?'

She stood beside the piano whilst he played one of Chopin's nocturnes. It was one that she knew and liked enormously. The music flowed out, lapping around her making her smile and, for the first time that day, forget Herbert.

'That was beautiful,' she cried, when his hands came to rest on the keys. 'I wish I could play like that. I wish it more than anything else in the world!' She knew that she could say such a thing to him, whereas if she said it to her mother she would be told not to be so silly. Not to exaggerate. How many times had she been told not to exaggerate in her life when she had merely been telling the truth?

'Is that true, Ellen?'

She nodded. He was obviously a man who could recognise truth.

'Would you like me to teach you? To give you lessons?'

She could not believe it. Was he, who played so beautifully, actually offering to teach *her*? But she couldn't accept. Why not? There was to be no question of payment or anything like that, he would do it because he wanted to, because he felt her desire to play was so strong and so important to her.

'If you do I won't allow you to pay me either.'

'Shall we strike a bargain? I will give you a daily lesson and you will give me my evening meal. I still think I come off best—'

'No!' How could he say such a thing!

They shook hands upon their bargain.

There was no point in wasting away time, was there? Nicolas got up and Ellen sat down on the red plush stool and laid her hands on the keys. They were trembling, just a little. But as she began to play her nervousness fled and the only thing she was conscious of was her pleasure in playing this piano. It was so mellow and harmonious compared with her own. She knew that it was time to get hers tuned again but she had been putting it off because of the difficulty of smuggling in the piano tuner without her mother knowing. She had to contact Isadora's piano tuner – Isadora's mother had bought her a piano when she was five but she had never advanced beyond Grade One – and arrange for him to come in time to finish well before her mother was due home in the afternoon. And then she had to scrape the money together to pay him.

Ellen had a natural talent, Nicolas was convinced of that. Her touch was good and he could feel the music inside her.

'Honest?'

'Why don't you believe what I say, Ellen? Do you think I would lie?'

35

She laughed. She felt so happy!

All the way home she hummed the Chopin nocturne.

Isadora was not in such a happy mood. She was leaning against the wall waiting for Ellen.

'Where have you been?'

Ellen smiled.

'I've been looking all over for you. For ages.'

Isadora wanted to talk about George. His attributes must be discussed backwards and forwards, as well as everything he had said to her so far. Isadora had a compulsion to voice all that went through her mind.

'What are you grinning about?' she demanded, breaking off in the middle of her recitation. 'Ellie Ferguson, what have you been up to?'

'Wouldn't you like to know?'

'Come on, tell me! You know we don't have any secrets from one another.'

'You may not have any from me, Issie, but I do have one or two I keep from you.'

Isadora did not believe it. She knew Ellen too well, she said. Anyway, what about the end of term dance? What about it? asked Ellen. She was going to go, wasn't she? said Isadora. She must go and make up a foursome with George and Isadora.

'A foursome? And who do you think's going to be number four?'

'What about Ginger McGuff?'

'You must be joking.'

'There's always Davie.'

'Davie? Don't be daft. He just about comes up to my waist.'

'Don't exaggerate, Ellie!'

The stair door opened and out came Davie carrying a football under his arm.

'Fancy a game, Ellie?'

Ellen went at once leaving Isadora to lean against the wall and sigh and wonder how she put up with having Ellie Ferguson as her best friend. Before long a crowd of small kids had appeared from out of stairs, basements and back greens to join the game. The street became filled with shouting, running, kicking children.

Old Granny Morrison's window went up with a rattle and she leant out at an alarming angle wearing a kind of dust cap and wrap-round overall. In her well-known voice that was showing no signs of weakening with age, she delivered a tirade down on to the heads below. It appeared she had a headache but no one wrapped up in the excitement of the game was at all interested in her sufferings. Mr Burns, who was sober and had stopped to watch and give the ball the odd, sly kick when it came his way, shouted up to her to give over and stop being such a sour puss, the kids were just enjoying themselves and not doing anybody any harm. Except for Granny Morrison. Her window went down with a thump and Isadora felt the vibrations in the back of her neck two storeys down.

Glancing round she saw her mother entering the street, her shoulders sagging under the weight of the muesli and wheat germ in her shopping bags. She had been to the health food shop.

'Isadora, come and give me a hand!'

As Isadora approached Mrs MacBain began her lecture on deportment, stressing that slouching against walls would do nothing for the spine, except deform it. She herself was currently crazy about yoga and was trying to persuade her daughter and Ellen to take it up. She paused now, having passed the bags to Isadora, to take a look at Ellen who was in the middle of heading the ball up the street to Davie. She shook her head. Football was a barbaric game and certainly quite unsuitable for girls.

'Och, Mum! You sound like Queen Victoria.'

Mrs MacBain swept on into her flat, inspired perhaps by the vision of that regal personage. Isadora humped the muesli and wheat germ in behind her.

And the kids played on till they were called in to tea.

Ellen had to go when her mother arrived. Mrs Ferguson was also carrying laden shopping bags and looked none too pleased at seeing her daughter playing football and yelling with the best of them. It was all right when she was younger, she said, when they got upstairs, but now that she was fourteen didn't she think it was time she put that behind her?

After they had eaten, Mrs Ferguson went out to meet Herbert who was taking her to the cinema. Ellen went to her room and sat down on the piano stool.

'Hi, Pa!' She saluted him. 'I met the nicest man today and he's the most fantastic pianist. Just about as good as you . . . but oh, no better! No one could be better than you. You'd like him, I know you would. His name is Nicolas.'

She began to play, to pick out the melody of the Chopin nocturne.

Next day she had another lesson with Nicolas which lasted for well over an hour and afterwards he went and sat by the window with his eyes closed whilst she played on and on. There was no reason why she should not stay and practise in his room, he said, if she was in no hurry to get home. She was not. Her mother knew where she was and thought it was nice that she should help the needy. Anyway, she herself was going to meet Herbert who was taking her for a drink in a cocktail bar.

Coming home as the May evening was beginning to darken and skeins of pink swathed the black rooftops, Ellen met Isadora who had been looking for her again.

'I thought you'd have been out with Georgie Porgie?'

'I was. But he had to go in early to do his homework.'

Ellen smiled. George would not last long, certainly not till the summer dance.

'Where have *you* been, Ellie? Don't be so mean! Have you been out on a date?'

Ellen danced away from her, laughing, taunting, teasing. Isadora advanced, demanding to be told.

'You have, haven't you? Who is he?'

'He's tall, dark and handsome. And that's all I'm going to tell you.'

'You're a close one, Ellie Ferguson,' said Isadora and flounced off into her house.

Ellen went upstairs humming her piece of Chopin.

Being so preoccupied with Nicolas and music had left her little time to think of Herbert. She did not think of him at all until the next afternoon after school. His name was brought up by Isadora who had an insatiable curiosity about anything which fell even vaguely into the category labelled romantic. To consider Herbert in terms of romance one would need to be very vague indeed, Ellen considered. Davie and Isadora were drinking coffee in her room.

'Do you think your mother's going to marry him?' asked Isadora in a dreamy voice which indicated that she was thinking of herself floating up some aisle in a cloud of white and not Mrs Ferguson.

Davie sat up, almost knocking over his coffee. He blinked rapidly several times in succession, a habit of his when he was startled. He had obviously never even considered the possibility of Ellen's mother becoming a bride again.

'Don't talk so daft,' said Ellen.

'He has a bungalow and your mother's always had a thing about a bungalow.'

'But not with a man in it.'

'You wouldn't go away and live on the other side of the town, would you, Ellie?' Davie looked even more startled.

'Of course not,' said Ellen crossly.

'But what if—'

Ellen cut across Isadora. There would be no ifs, she was going to stay here in this flat where she had lived

39

all her life. Her mother might think that marrying Herbert was a possibility – though why she would want to apart from the bungalow was a mystery – but Ellen was convinced that Herbert would not want her along as a stepdaughter. And her mother couldn't just abandon her, at least not before she was sixteen.

'When you're sixteen you could marry your tall, dark, handsome stranger,' said Isadora.

Davie blinked again. 'Tall, dark—'

'Ask Ellie who's tall and dark.'

'No wonder I don't tell you everything, Isadora MacBain!'

'You see, Davie, Ellie has a boyfriend. Surprise, surprise! Isn't she the dark horse? She goes to meet him every day—'

Isadora fled from Ellen's wrath and departed laughing all the way down the stairs. Ellen slammed the door on the sound.

'Pay no attention to her, Davie.'

Davie said he'd need to be off too as they were having their tea early. His dad was going to the dogs with his Uncle Harry.

Ellen sat alone by the window staring down at the washing flapping on the back green. A sprightly wind was lifting it. And all around the grass rectangle bloomed flowers cultivated by Mr Mellon who had green fingers. They did have a garden, the only difference between theirs and Herbert's being that they had to share it, which she for one did not mind. But she knew that her mother did.

On Thursday which was late night shopping – although not at Mrs Ferguson's shop – she took Ellen up to Princes Street for a pair of shoes which Ellen did not want.

'They're real nice, Ellen,' said her mother as she and the shop assistant bent over a pair of black patent leather shoes in admiration. Ellen stared above their

40

heads at the boxes lining the wall. She hated shoe shops. 'Make your feet look smaller.'

'But they'll make me look taller.'

'Nonsense! We'll take them,' said Mrs Ferguson to the shop assistant.

They had high heels, which was Ellen's main objection. Small heels, insisted Mrs Ferguson, no more than a couple of inches. But those were two inches which she couldn't afford to have added to her, Ellen wailed all the way home. Once home, Mrs Ferguson raked in Ellen's wardrobe and hauled out a number of cotton dresses only one of which Ellen could squeeze into.

'It's quite a nice wee dress, you know,' said Mrs Ferguson, tugging it around Ellen's waist.

'I can hardly breathe.'

'Nonsense! Anyway, I can let it out half an inch.'

'Half an inch!'

It was let out the half inch and down one but even then barely covered her knees.

'I'm a ghastly looking sight,' said Ellen on Saturday surveying herself in the mirror when they had a dress rehearsal for Herbert's tea party. 'The Mad Herbert's tea party.' 'What was that you said?' 'Nothing.' Her mother had insisted on her going to the hairdresser's that morning where they had thinned and set her hair. Isadora, whom she had met on the way home, had run off along the street in paroxysms of laughter. Davie had merely blinked, but very rapidly and repeatedly, until Ellen had wanted to scream. She had left him standing on the landing looking like a dazed rabbit caught in the glare of headlights.

On Sunday morning Ellen woke up with a sore throat.

'I can't go,' she said hoarsely. 'It wouldn't be fair to Herbert. I might give him my germs. He doesn't look like the type who would welcome germs.'

'Nonsense!' said her mother, opening up her

medicine cupboard and taking out an assortment of remedies.

They set off just after three. Best to leave on the early side, said Mrs Ferguson, since the buses were none too reliable on a Sunday. And they had to take two, one to Princes Street and another from there to Herbert's suburb. They would normally have walked up town but there was the matter of Ellen's shoes, as well as Mrs Ferguson's which were also new. They squeaked as she walked but Ellen forbore to mention it.

Isadora and Davie were in the street to watch them go. ·

'Have a nice time, Ellie,' called out Isadora.

Ellen walked past with head held erect and tripped on the edge of a cracked paving stone.

'Pick your feet up, dear,' said her mother.

The first bus came quite quickly and deposited them on Princes Street where they stood for almost twenty minutes waiting for the second. Whilst they stood Ellen eyed the Sunday strollers enviously. They had nothing else to do but parade up and down Princes Street, stop off for an ice-cream in the gardens, listen to the speakers on their soap boxes beside the gallery, feed the pigeons, sit on a seat for a while, admire the flowers and watch the world go by. Or they might hang over the railing and idly wait for the cuckoo to come out of his garland of flowers and announce the hour. Or they might walk up the Mound to the castle and look down on the city from its ramparts, or walk down the Royal Mile to Holyrood Palace. There were all sorts of things to do other than visit Herbert in his bungalow.

The bus came.

They would have quite a long ride, said Mrs Ferguson cheerfully, so they might as well go up to the top deck, something she usually did not do because of the smell of tobacco smoke. They were to get off one stop before the terminus. Ellen allowed her to sit beside the window since she seemed so interested in the route they were about to traverse. Mrs Ferguson commented on the sunny day and the people in their summer clothes in the streets and then, when they had travelled far enough, on the trees and flowers in the gardens. She enthused greatly on the gardens. The cherry trees were in full bloom, and the lilacs, and the laburnums.

'Aren't they absolutely beautiful, Ellen?'

Ellen grunted, refusing to allow herself the pleasure of looking at the frothy pink blossoms and hanging golden branches. She had been in the Botanic Garden the day before and wandered under the trees bewitched by their beauty. She had told Nicolas about them and he had asked her to describe everything she had seen in detail so that he might refresh his memory and see them again in his mind's eye. She wished that she were on her way to Nicolas now. She sighed, fairly loudly.

'You will try, won't you, Ellen?'

'What do you mean – try?'

'You *know*! You weren't born yesterday.'

Her mother was watching the road carefully, face pressed against the dusty window. In her hand she held a sheet of paper covered with Herbert's instructions. His writing was like himself: small, neat, cramped.

'Come on, Ellen! This is it.'

They were the last two people on the bus, bar one. A solitary man remained to make the last lap of the journey. They alighted, the bus moved off. Ellen turned to survey the terrain. No stout grey tenements reared to meet the sky here. They had arrived in the land of bungalows.

FOUR

'Are you sure we're still in Edinburgh?' asked Ellen, tugging irritably at her dress. The waist kept twisting and was exceedingly uncomfortable. She couldn't wait till she got home and pulled on her old jeans again. And her feet hurt already with only a small part of the outing accomplished.

Mrs Ferguson did not deign to answer. She led the way purposefully onward, clutching the piece of paper, smiling and inhaling the fresh air in deep draughts, declaring that it was marvellous to breathe in such air after the foul air of the street. She meant *their* street.

Herbert, it seemed, lived miles from the bus stop as well as miles from the city centre. They turned down one street after another, all similar, lined with bungalows fronted with neat gardens. There was scarcely a soul in sight. 'What do people do out here?' asked Ellen.

'They lead decent lives. They dig their gardens, grow flowers. Oh, look, Ellen, aren't the roses simply beautiful?'

They paused so that Mrs Ferguson could admire them at closer range and drink in a whiff of their perfume. They were not Herbert's roses, not yet. No, Mrs Ferguson was sure they had not missed the way, she was following Herbert's instructions to the letter and he had charted every bend in the road most meticulously. But they should soon be there. First on the left, second on the right. . . .

Ellen's right heel felt as if it was on fire. She was sure she must have a blister the size of an egg on it, as well as a thick, red weal around her middle.

44

They turned into the second on the right.

'Isn't this a lovely street?' cried Mrs Ferguson.

Ellen did not reply. It was a narrower street than some of the others they had trekked through and the houses were more cramped together. It looked as if some builder in the thirties had bought a piece of land and tried to see how many semi-detached bungalows he could squash on to it. He had been quite an inventive man.

'So quiet,' sighed Mrs Ferguson.

'I'd call it dead. Stone cold dead.'

Ellen could call it what she liked but Mrs Ferguson liked peace and quiet, especially after having to put up with kids playing football and yelling in the street and Old Granny Morrison screaming out of her upstairs window. It was highly unlikely that people would ever scream out of windows here.

'They wouldn't have the energy,' said Ellen. She was beginning to suspect that everyone was asleep.

'The quality of life is not dependent on the amount of noise one can make. Quite the reverse! Oh, look, there's Herbert!'

Mrs Ferguson waved with a kind of girlish excitement that Ellen had never seen in her before. She was behaving more and more like Isadora every minute. And there indeed was Herbert and he was waving back from his sitting-room window where he had been seated awaiting their arrival.

He came to the front door of his bungalow to meet them. Two steps up the garden path and they were there. The front garden was like a postage stamp; four rose bushes fought for possession.

'Welcome to "Ben Nevis",' said Herbert.

'Ben Nevis?' said Ellen.

'It's the name of the house.' He looked a little sheepish. 'Mother went to Fort William on her honeymoon, you see. She looked out on Ben Nevis from her window.'

'Did she go with your father?'

'Ellen!' reproved Mrs Ferguson.

They went inside.

The sitting room, which was about half the size of theirs at home, was crammed with large pieces of heavy brown furniture around which they had to squeeze in order to reach the three-piece moquette suite grouped about the half-moon rug in front of the fireplace. The material proved scratchy to Ellen's bare legs and her dress being short did not offer much protection. She sat in one of the armchirs with her legs sticking out across the rust coloured half-moon rug. She felt she dwarfed the room and yet she was silenced by it. It was all quite strange to her. She glanced about in awe. On the top of every surface stood china ornaments encrusted with flowers and ringed with gilt and then there were sepia photographs of ancient looking men and women and pieces of brass (ugh, she hated brass). Three plaster ducks flew across the wall heading towards the window as if they wanted to seek refuge in the damask drapes. Ellen let her eyes rove freely, for Herbert and her mother were preoccupied with one another tossing pleasantries to and fro. Her eye stopped on a large framed photograph which held pride of place on the sideboard. Without a doubt it was Herbert's mother.

'Shall we have some tea?' said Herbert. 'The kettle's just on the boil. No, sit still, Rose, it's my treat today.'

'What a lovely room,' said Mrs Ferguson, when he had gone to make the tea. She would not meet Ellen's eye.

Herbert was back very soon pushing a three-tiered tea trolley.

'My goodness, Herbert, you have been busy!' Mrs Ferguson jumped up to assist. It took a bit of manoeuvring to get the trolley on to the half-moon rug.

Herbert went back to the kitchen to fetch the tray with his mother's silver tea set.

'What a lovely tea set!' said Mrs Ferguson.

'Suppose it was your mother's wedding tea set?' said Ellen.

It was.

Herbert poured tea from his mother's tea pot into her fine china cups. Her wedding china. It was still intact, after forty years.

'Be careful now, Ellen,' said her mother, her eye fixed anxiously on her daughter. 'And sit up, dear, do!'

Ellen sat up and her foot caught the trolley making it tremble and all the plates of cake upon it. Mrs Ferguson steadied it with both hands and repeated her admonition.

It was all right, said Herbert; no harm done. He passed around the sandwiches of fish paste and cheese spread which Mrs Ferguson found delicious. Ellen said no thank you, she wasn't hungry.

'A piece of cake then, Ellen? I can recommend my mother's fruit cake.'

'Your mother's fruit cake?'

'It was the last one she baked before she died.'

'Fruit cake does keep a long time, Ellen,' put in Mrs Ferguson hurriedly. 'It can last for years.'

'Did she bake it just before she died?'

'Two days before. "There's a cake in the tin, Herbert", she said to me.'

'Were those her dying words?'

'Ellen!' said her mother.

'Not exactly,' said Herbert. 'Almost though. Almost.'

'How interesting!' said Ellen. 'Fancy thinking about cake just before you die.'

'I would love a piece, thank you, Herbert,' said Mrs Ferguson.

The cake was pronounced to be delicious and beautifully moist, but Ellen still declined. It was like being offered cake from the dead, she said later to Isadora. Anyway, she was not much of a cake hand, as she explained to Herbert; she took after her father who hated sweet things.

'Your mother was a handsome woman, Herbert,' put in Mrs Ferguson quickly — she spent half the afternoon putting in quick remarks. She glanced over at the photograph.

Herbert nodded. She had had a very strong character too. Yes, said Mrs Ferguson, one could tell that just from looking at her picture.

'You mean by the glint in her eye?' said Ellen.

Mrs Ferguson sent Ellen another of her censorious glances before turning her attention to the china and other ornaments. All were duly admired. And then she discovered the china cabinet which was lurking behind the settee. She got up to examine the array of dishes displayed behind the locked glass. It was all Herbert's mother's wedding china. Mrs Ferguson sighed and appeared lost in admiration.

'Have you any of your wedding china left, Mum? Or did I break it all?'

Ellen laughed; Herbert gave a nervous little smile; Mrs Ferguson frowned. Now that Ellen came to think of it she could not remember her mother ever having wedding china. She was just as well without it if it usually came like the stuff in the glass cupboard. Dead china: that was what that was.

Ellen stretched her legs again and set the plates a-rattling. Herbert lifted the trolley out apologising, saying that his room must seem very small to them after their large one.

'Our rooms are far too big,' said Mrs Ferguson. 'They're too difficult to heat properly.'

'I love big rooms. Dad did too, didn't he? He needed space to stretch out in. It was he who wanted the flat, wasn't it?'

'More tea, Rose?' asked Herbert.

She would love a little more: it was such delicious tea. Ellen thought she would scream if her mother uttered the word 'delicious' one more time. Herbert discovered the pot was dry and went off to replenish it in spite of Mrs Ferguson's assurances that he should not bother.

'How kind he is! You might at least have made an effort, Ellen! You didn't eat anything. After he'd gone to all that trouble.'

Ellen pointed out that Herbert hadn't eaten much of anything the other night in their house after her mother had gone to all that trouble. Mrs Ferguson was momentarily taken aback but rallied.

'And I wish you didn't have to mention your father every two minutes.'

'Why shouldn't I—'

'You know perfectly well why not.'

'Anyway, he mentions his mother.' They looked over at the photograph on the sideboard. Herbert's mother, hair swept up in imperious Edwardian style – although she could not of course have been an Edwardian, – gazed levelly at them. 'She looks a bit like Old Granny Morrison. Around the mouth.'

Mrs Ferguson's own mouth twitched. 'Shush, for goodness' sake!' She got up and went to the window and when Herbert returned she set about admiring the street thus giving Herbert an opportunity to enthuse on the neighbourhood. It was nice and it was quiet and you got a nice class of person living here. His mother had come here as a bride and in the back room had given birth to Herbert so Herbert had many years of memories to dwell upon.

'I know it might not be very adventurous of me,' he said apologetically, 'but I'd be quite happy to spend the rest of my days here.'

There was nothing wrong with that, said Mrs Ferguson. To be happy was the main thing, wasn't it? They smiled at one another.

Ellen jumped up unable to tolerate the afternoon any longer. Could she go now? 'Go?' repeated her mother. Ellen began to gabble. She had her history project to finish for the morning and a French essay and maths and she had to practise the 'cello. She searched desperately for further possibilities.

'Oh, all right! Although you should have been doing all that earlier instead of playing football in the street.' Would Herbert mind if Ellen went now? Mrs Ferguson herself would stay a little longer: she was dying to have another piece of that delicious cake and stroll around the garden. That was fine by him, said Herbert.

Ellen waved to them through the window as she passed by the bungalow. She walked as far as the corner and then when she was safely on the other side broke into a run. Blisters or no blisters, she would run all the way to the bus stop and all the way home if no bus came.

A bus did come and took her back to Princes Street. When she alighted there and struck up Frederick Street she felt she could breathe again. She was back on her own side. She walked home crossing George Street and Queen Street then going steadily downhill. The views over to Fife were spectacular and there was not a bungalow to be seen.

As she turned into the street she heard Davie's voice. She scuttled round the corner quickly just as the ball was coming in her direction. She lifted her foot and met it straight on with the toe of her new patent leather shoe. The ball soared clean over the heads of the nearer children and landed neatly right in front of Davie's feet.

'Good shot, Ellie!'

George was playing too, as well as three or four other larger boys. The game was fast and furious and the smaller kids ran to and fro bleating with complaints about not getting a chance. Isadora was leaning against the wall eating a bright pink toffee apple.

At half-time they took a break and George and Isadora went to buy ice-creams. Davie and Ellen rested sitting on the pavement with their feet in the gutter. Ellen surveyed her new shoes. They would never be the same again, that was for sure.

'I like your garden party outfit.'

50

Davie ducked as her hand came out. He was brilliant when it came to ducking. It was because he was so small, Ellen liked to tell him.

After the refreshments they resumed playing. As she reached for a wide ball, Ellen felt her dress rip somewhere in the region of the armhole but carried on not caring about that. It was the last time she would ever wear it.

A ball was travelling fast towards her. She brought her foot up and as it contacted the ball her shoe was tossed up into the air. Her new black patent leather shoe with a small heel. At once George was on it grabbing it between two hands like a rugby ball. 'Right, Davie!' he shouted. The football lay forgotten in the gutter. The boys zigzagged up and down the street, rugby fashion, alternately clutching and passing Ellen's shoe. Ellen sat down on the kerb and began to laugh.

Her laughter dried with the arrival of her mother in the street. She was walking tenderly for her own new shoes were now pinching her toes and she was carrying before her a bunch of roses from Herbert's garden. Davie, who had hold of Ellen's shoe at this particular moment, faltered, dropped it, and then stood transfixed, gazing at the stiff retreating back of Ellen's mother.

Ellen retrieved her shoe and followed her mother into the lobby and up the three flights of stairs. Not a word was said. Mrs Ferguson walked very erect with Ellen behind, her eyes on the back of her mother's heels. They looked inflamed even through their nylon covering.

They went into the flat and Ellen closed the door. Her mother laid down the roses, winced, and for a brief second paused to suck her finger before kicking her shoes across the hall. She turned to look at Ellen. Her tongue loosened then. Did Ellen think she had money to burn? Did Ellen know how much those shoes had cost? Well, of course she did since she had been there, hadn't she? But she had never wanted the ridiculous shoes. Black patent leather with a two-inch heel! And she had never wanted to wear this stupid dress or go to stupid Herbert's.

'That's enough! When *do* you think you're going to start acting your age?'

How did one start acting one's age? asked Ellen. Were there directions written up somewhere? Rules to follow? Her mother told her not to be so impudent.

Ellen went into her room and sat down at the piano. She gave her father only a silent greeting before she started to play. He knew there were times when she didn't feel like talking. She played her own tune, 'The Gooseberry'.

> 'They call me the gooseberry
> 'Cos I'm always alone
> Walking one on the outside—'

The door opened behind her.

'What are you playing, dear?' The tone of her mother's voice had changed completely from the moment before.

'Nothing.'

'Would you like a cup of tea? I'm just going to make one.'

'All right.'

When Ellen went to the kitchen she found her mother standing by the sink looking out at the sky. The kettle was about to boil. Ellen lifted it, infused the tea. Her mother seemed oblivious of the boiling kettle, or even of her presence. She continued to stare out at the white wispy clouds that trailed across the bright blue above the rooftops. They had been having an unusually long spell of early summer weather. Ellen wondered, aloud, how long it was going to last. She received no answer.

'Tea's ready, Mum. Shall I pour it?'

'Let's take it through to the front room, shall we?'

In the front room they could hear the children quite clearly in the street. Before they went to Herbert's

Mrs Ferguson had opened the window a few inches to air the room out.

'I thought I might make some lasagne this evening, just for the two of us. Would you like that, Ellen?'

'Oh, I would!' Ellen felt so happy she could have somersaulted across the room except that that would have upset her mother. She felt as if a stone had been lifted from her heart. Things were going to be as they had always been. On Sunday evenings her mother often made something Ellen especially liked; she would open a bottle of wine for herself and give Ellen a glass, and she would set the table by the window with candles and gaily coloured serviettes.

'I'm sorry, Mum, about the shoes.'

'It's all right, dear. I've forgiven you! I know I shouldn't make you wear things you don't like. Come and sit down, love. I want to talk to you.'

Ellen's elation dimmed, the desire to somersault vanished. People wanting to talk to you usually forebode nothing good. She heard Davie call to George below and wished she was back down there with them chasing the ball. Her mother was patting the seat of the sofa indicating that she wished Ellen to come and sit there, beside her. Ellen did as requested and took a drink of tea to warm and quieten her stomach.

Mrs Ferguson began by sighing. This was not going to be easy and Ellen must try to be understanding. She said that their lives had been none too easy since they had been left on their own.

'I've been quite happy,' burst out Ellen.

Mrs Ferguson sighed again. They had always had problems over money, she pointed out, and there were times too when she had been lonely, Ellen must realise that. Ellen stared at her bare and none too clean feet, which normally her mother would have commented on. She realised only one thing. She looked up at her mother's face.

'You're not going to marry Herbert, are you? Just

so as you'll have no more money problems and won't be lonely?'

It was not as simple as that, said Mrs Ferguson, picking her words carefully. She was very fond of Herbert and he of her and they had a lot in common.

'What?' demanded Ellen.

'We are both people alone.'

'You have me.'

'You will go, Ellen. Oh, yes, you will! And then in a few years' time—'

Where did her mother think she was going to go to? She intended to work in Edinburgh when she left school, or if she went to university she would go to the one here. She would never think of leaving Edinburgh or this street. Never!

'You can't be that narrow, Ellen.'

'Why not? If I'm happy here.'

'You might get married.'

'Don't talk daft!'

'Why not?'

Ellen shrugged, unwilling to talk about the possibility of herself getting married. It was enough to have to talk about her mother marrying.

'I'm confident that Herbert will make you a good father, dear. He's a most kind and considerate man.'

'I don't want a father. I've got one.'

'Now, Ellen, please—'

'How can you bear to think of marrying Herbert after being married to Dad?'

There were a lot of things about her previous marriage Ellen did not understand and one day Mrs Ferguson intended to speak to her more fully. But now she must ask Ellen to accept the fact that she intended to marry Herbert. Yes, she did! He had proposed and she had accepted. For once in her life she wanted to live in a nice house with a garden and have her own front door. She spoke strongly. She was sick of this old flat where they could hear the mice scrabbling about at nights behind the wainscoting, sick of the dirty stair smelling of cats and heaven knows what else, especially on a Saturday night when folk had been drinking overmuch in the pub, sick of Granny Morrison and a good few others who were too numerous to mention!

Ellen was staring at her round-eyed with horror. 'You wouldn't sell the flat, would you? You wouldn't!'

'I'm afraid I'll have to, love,' said Mrs Ferguson gently. 'Well, of course! We couldn't expect Herbert to come and live here, could we?'

'You mean we're going to live in Herbert's bungalow?'

FIVE

'I have no intention of going to live away out there,' said Ellen to Nicolas. 'It's about fifty miles from the city centre. I'd just as soon go to the moon. Rather.'

But would she have the choice? asked Nicolas. When her mother married and sold the flat she would have to go, wouldn't she? He did sympathise though: it was not a happy experience to have to leave all your friends and go to live in unknown surroundings. He knew all about that. But he knew too that there were times when you must just accept and make the best of it.

'It was different for you though, wasn't it? I mean, it was war and stuff. A matter of life and death.'

'Indeed, yes.' Nicolas smiled. 'And this is a matter of love and marriage.'

'Love?' echoed Ellen. 'She's only marrying him for security.'

Nicolas's smile widened. He shrugged, spread out his hands. Didn't he believe her? How could one know? he countered.

'Anyway, she's not married yet and the flat's not sold yet.'

'You'll have to face up to it sooner or later, Ellen.'

'We'll see,' said Ellen, wanting to say no more on the topic at the moment. She and Isadora and Davie were having a council of war later — it was just like the old days when they were small — to discuss what could be done. They were all agreed upon one thing: *something* had to be done. 'Move away, Ellie?' Isadora had said. 'You can't.' 'The street wouldn't be the same,' said Davie.

It was time now for Ellen's lesson. She had been practising diligently and Nicolas was delighted with her progress. He used to teach when he was younger but no pupil he had ever had matched Ellen. Yes, honestly! He felt sure she could become a professional musician if she wanted to. She would want to. Oh yes, she would! Then her excitement dimmed a little. There was the question of her mother who hated pianos and piano players. She sighed now. Perhaps one day, after her mother was married to Herbert and settled down, Nicolas might be able to talk to her and persuade her? He would be willing to try.

'She is *not* going to marry Herbert. And I don't think talking to her would do any good. It's like an allergy she has. She comes out in a rash when I play the piano!'

The subject was dropped. They concluded the lesson and Nicolas went back to his chair leaving her to continue with her practice. He was almost asleep by the time she finished.

Yawning and stretching, she got up from the piano stool. Her arms were tired and her neck stiff. She must hurry now and get back to the street where Isadora and Davie would be waiting. Glancing idly at the photographs grouped on a shelf on the back wall, her eye was arrested by one of a young man. Strangely, she had not noticed it before. He was smiling, this young man, with eyes that were

56

incredibly like Nicolas's. And he was tall, dark and handsome.

'Who is this, Nicolas? The dark young man leaning against the wall?'

'Oh, that is my nephew Nick, my sister's boy.'

Ellen examined the photograph more closely. He was very like his uncle. 'Where does he live?'

'Paris.'

'He looks nice.'

'He is. I am very fond of him.'

'Does he ever come and visit you?'

'Sometimes.'

'What age is he?'

Nicolas had to think, to calculate backwards. Eighteen, he thought, or perhaps nineteen. Eighteen. Four years older than she was, five at most. She wished he would come to Edinburgh for she was sure she would like him if he was at all like Nicolas.

The little French clock on the mantelpiece pinged eight times. She put the photograph back on the shelf.

'Where on earth have you been?' asked Isadora. 'We've been waiting for hours. I'm sick of waiting for you, Ellie Ferguson. You deserve to move to a bungalow on the south side.'

'My apologies! I had an important assignation.' Ellen bowed from the waist and wondered if Nicolas's nephew would bow. He looked like the kind of young man who might. Certainly Nicolas would have done when he was young.

Apologies did not console Isadora although being taken into Ellen's confidence might have done. She plied her with questions as they mounted the stairs. What was he called? Where did he live? How old was he? Davie came behind saying nothing.

When Ellen opened the door of her flat they heard a flurry of laughter billowing out from the sitting room, and then another.

'It's your mother's chums,' said Isadora. 'We watched them all coming in.'

Isadora and Davie went ahead into Ellen's room whilst she went to see her mother.

'Come in and say hello to the girls, Ellen,' cried Mrs Ferguson gaily. They were drinking champagne and eating cheese footballs.

'Hello,' said Ellen.

'Been at Nicolas's, have you?' said Mavis, who had had her hair rinsed a kind of purplish-blue colour. 'Isn't he sweet?'

'Isn't it wonderful news, Ellen?' said Netta. Ellen stared. 'Your mother going to be married of course?'

'Ellen's still getting used to the idea,' said Mrs Ferguson with a little laugh.

'You're a lucky girl, Ellen,' said Olive. 'You're going to have a lovely home, from what your mother tells us. Really lovely.'

Ellen withdrew. As soon as she closed the door her mother, she knew, would lower her voice and confide in the girls, telling them how difficult Ellen was being and they would reassure her. Giver her time, Rose!

Time would do nothing to make her like Herbert, she informed Davie and Isadora, who had made themselves comfortable on the floor cushions in her room. Davie had brought a bottle of lemonade and three chocolate biscuits. Herbert sounded a right twit, observed Isadora, with his tea trolley and his mother's fruit cake. Davie handed out the biscuits and offered Ellen the first drink of the lemonade. She tilted the bottle up, took a long swig, wiped the top and passed it to Isadora. And now they must think, declared Davie.

Isadora had the first suggestion. She was always quick at thinking things up and never paused to see if they were feasible or not before voicing them. Ellen could have a nervous breakdown and the doctor would say she couldn't be moved. Davie was sceptical. How could she convince the doctor she was having a nervous breakdown? He might be daft but he wasn't that daft.

'She's good at acting. And fooling about.'

'I could take to my bed.'

'And refuse to eat.'

Ellen was not so sure that she fancied that. She took another bite of her chocolate biscuit. Isadora did not mean that she should really starve, they would smuggle food in to her. They would soon cotton on to that, said Davie.

'You have to throw cold water on everything,' snapped Isadora.

'We've got to be realistic. The plan's got to work, hasn't it? If she really stopped eating she'd get thin and feel weak.'

'Until I could hardly lift my head from the pillow.' Ellen let her head flop about. She was beginning to feel a little weak, come to think of it. She took another bite and the biscuit was gone. Then she had another drink from the lemonade bottle. Davie and Isadora were arguing about whether she could or could not fool them by pretending to fade away. Isadora said it wouldn't do her any harm to stop eating for a few days, it was one way of slimming. Ellen took another drink telling herself she needed the sustenance and never mind the calories. There were some girls at school who took a delight in telling you how many calories you'd taken on every time you ate a bite. They always seemed to be standing beside the chocolate vending machine.

Isadora had another think. 'You could chain yourself to the railings, Ellie. The stair railings. That might be fun.'

'For you, Issie, maybe, but not for me. I don't know if I'd fancy languishing in chains.'

She would fancy less languishing in a bungalow on the south side, retorted Isadora. True. Ellen sighed. Perhaps she should listen more carefully to Isadora's ideas. Desperation made one resort to all sorts of strange things. Chains could be sawn through, Davie reminded them.

'You know your trouble, Davie Dunlop?' said Isadora. 'You have no imagination. So OK then, if you don't like my ideas, you think of something! Hey, Ellie, don't finish *all* the lemonade!'

Davie said he was trying to think if only they could shut up for a minute. He rested his chin on his hands. The trouble was that Ellie being under age meant that her mother could force her to go with her or else she'd be taken off to some sort of remand home or other. That might be better than having to live with Herbert and his mother, said Ellen. His mother? Wasn't his mother dead? asked Isadora, taking hold of the bottle. 'That's all you think!' said Ellen darkly.

She could always run away. That was a course of action that had occurred to her many times since first meeting Herbert. Where would she think of running to? Isadora wanted to know. London perhaps. Why not London? It was a big city and the police would have a hard time tracking you down there. Now if you went to Perth or Fort William – Fort William. Ben Nevis. Yes, perhaps running away was not at all a bad idea. Isadora said she wouldn't mind coming with her if she was going to London. She fancied a spell in the big city. They could live in Chelsea. 'Ha, ha!' said Davie. They could take Granny Morrison's cat and carry their worldly goods over their shoulder in a bundle, said Ellen, and when they entered the city the church bells would start to ring.

'Will you never be serious, Ellie Ferguson?' said Isadora.

'I am.' Ellen opened her wide eyes innocently. 'All the time.'

In Davie's view if you had to go to London you might as well go to the south side of Edinburgh; at least you could come back to the street for a visit from time to time. But she did not intend to leave the street *at all*, said Ellen.

'We'll just have to block the sale of the flat then,' he said.

'Good idea,' said Isadora. 'But how?'

'For a start, Ellie, you can put folk off.'

'That should be easy,' said Isadora, bending backwards out of Ellen's reach.

But Davie was being serious for Ellen would probably have to show some prospective purchasers round whilst her mother was out at work. She could slip in some damning remarks, in a casual sort of way of course. Don't worry about that funny looking stain on the wall, I'm sure it's only damp. No it couldn't possibly be dry rot, I'm sure it couldn't. Dry rot was the worst possible thing to find in old property, according to Davie; she would only have to say the magic words and they would all disappear down the stairs like greased lightning.

'They might even jump over the banisters in case they got contaminated,' giggled Isadora. She sobered and suggested that they make out a list of horribles for Ellen to work from. Ellen fetched a piece of paper and a pen and wrote them down with many flourishes and twirls, in some cases adding illustrations.

Dry rot, wet rot, settlement, woodworm (it would always be possible to drill a few likely-looking holes), mice (infestations which came out at night), noisy neighbours (Davie could oblige with noise), dirty neighbours (Davie could oblige in this category too), suspected psychopath in the basement next door (Mr Burns), troublemaker below (Old Granny Morrison), suspicion that the flat is haunted. This last idea was of course Isadora's who would think about it and elaborate for Ellen the next day in chemistry over the bunsen burners. It was a formidable list. Davie said she must beware of mentioning everything, or even almost everything, to the same people. Credibility could only be stretched so far.

There would be times when her mother would be attending to the viewers herself, Ellen reminded him. What then? It was hardly likely that her mother could be induced to read out the list. Isadora giggled again. When Mrs Ferguson was at home their only option would be to fix the stair, said Davie. What did he have in mind? asked Isadora. Barricading it? Stretching barbed wire across the bottom? Locking the bottom door? That might be an idea. If people couldn't get it open after three tries they would just give up and go off; they weren't going to persist further when there were plenty of other properties on the market. Then after they had gone they could nip down and unlock it and no one would be any the wiser.

'Not foolproof.' Davie frowned. 'No, we'll need to dirty up the stair itself.'

'Make it look like a slum, you mean?' said Ellen. 'My mum's always saying that it is one.'

'Your mum's never seen a real slum,' said Davie, sounding worldly wise.

'You're right there. I must remember to tell her that.'

Her mother looked round the door at that moment but had obviously not heard a word for she was smiling. She wondered if they would like some apple juice and sandwiches and a piece of pizza? She said, 'Hello, Isadora, how are you, dear?' and 'Hello, Davie, nice to see you,' as if she hadn't seen them for months. Ellen went with her to fetch their snack. 'Hey, your mum looks really loopy about that Herbert,' said Isadora when she came back. 'About his bungalow, you should say,' Ellen corrected her.

She cut the pizza into three and divided up the sandwiches. At least they were getting some sort of bonus from her mother's happiness. When they were quiet and eating they could hear peals of laughter coming from the next room.

'They're getting stoned out of their minds,' said Ellen. 'Imagine becoming delirious over a bungalow on the south side with four rose bushes in the front garden.'

'You always exaggerate,' said Davie.

'Me? You must be joking.'

Ellen jumped to her feet.

'You've got to measure me, Issie. You haven't done it this week.'

Isadora groaned and asked if she couldn't have a minute's peace. The answer was no for Ellen was pulling the box from under the bed and getting out the ruler. She went and stood straight against the wall, not cheating. Both Isadora and Davie did the honours together this time, their feet pressed side by side on the box.

'Five feet eleven,' they both announced simultaneously.

'And not a centimetre over,' added Davie.

'Fantastic! Do you know I haven't grown *at all* in the last four months? Maybe I've stopped growing.' Ellen did a few ballet steps across the room, ending up collapsed on to the piano stool. She looked up at her father's smiling face. 'Isn't that good, Pa? I haven't grown at all!'

Davie and Isadora glanced at one another, Isadora rolled her eyes and Davie shrugged.

'Desirable top flat, convenient for city centre,' the advertisement began. 'Light, with good open outlook.' It went on to list the accommodation: sitting room, kitchen, etc. Ellen read it over Davie's shoulder. As soon as he had got his batch of evening papers he had hurried along the street and met her coming to meet him. Viewing was to be between four and five in the afternoon and seven and eight in the evening. It was necessary to have some daytime viewing, Mrs Ferguson said, so she would have to ask Ellen to be sure to be in during that hour.

The previous evening had seen a flurry of activity in their flat. Mrs Ferguson had vacuumed the carpets and washed and polished the kitchen floor and Ellen had been given the paintwork to wash down in the bathroom and kitchen, as well as all the grubby fingerprints to wipe off the walls. Her mother pointed out that most of them were beyond her reach. Since she could walk Ellen had had an infuriating habit of leaping up in the air and clutching at the walls on her downward journey. She certainly would not be able to do that in Herbert's bungalow! Indeed she would not, agreed Ellen: the ceilings were far too low. If she stretched her arms above her head she was positive she could touch them.

It was five minutes to four as Ellen and Davie stood in the street reading the advertisement. Ellen had come home from school quickly that day leaving Isadora and George to meander around the Water of Leith. She had suggested to Davie in the English class that morning that one way might be simply not to be home between four and five and then the people would just go away. But come back in the evening, he said, and complain to her mother. Davie was useful to try out ideas on: he was good at seeing the flaw, something Ellen herself usually missed in the heat of the excitement of having the idea.

'Good luck,' said Davie solemnly before leaving on his paper round.

Ellen sat on the piano stool waiting for viewers. She did not play. Her ears were pricked for the sound of the bell and once she got up thinking she heard it but opened the door to find the landing empty. There was not a sound on the stair either. Perhaps no one was interested in their desirable flat.

'Don't worry, Pa,' she told him. 'I won't let them put us out.'

At half-past four the bell rang unmistakably. Heart thumping, she went to the door. The Onion Johnny was resting against the banister, red cheeked and puffing, holding out a string of onions. Mrs Ferguson usually bought a string when he called. Ellen went to fetch the money from the tin in the kitchen marked 'Sundries'.

Five minutes later the first viewer came. A man. He, too, was puffing, like the Onion Johnny. He had a heart condition, he said; he could never cope with these stairs but since he was here he might as well take a look around. Ellen refrained from asking why he had bothered to come at all since the ad had said 'top flat'. She took him from room to room saying, 'This is the sitting room' and 'This is the bathroom.' There was no point in wasting the dry rot treatment on him.

'You'll never get your price,' he said as he took his leave.

She made a face at the back of the door.

Five minutes before the end of the viewing hour she had her second caller. She brightened when she saw the young woman on the doorstep holding a fat baby on her left hip and carrying a push chair under her right arm. There should not be much need to deter this one: the stairs would have already done that.

'It's a long way up,' said the woman.

'And your baby looks a ton weight,' said Ellen sympathetically, ushering her in.

'He'll soon be walking though, won't you, Daniel? He's nearly a year.'

Ellen took her first into the kitchen.

'Nice big working kitchen. I can't stand titchy ones.'

They went next to Ellen's bedroom.

'What a lovely proportioned room!'

'I don't think that stain's anything,' began Ellen, pointing to a blotch above the bed.

'Oh, I'm sure it isn't.' The woman touched it. 'Perfectly dry.'

Then they went to the sitting room.

'Isn't this lovely? You've got very good cornices, I must say, all intact. And it's so light.' She turned a beaming smile upon Ellen. 'I just adore top flats. It gives you such a marvellous feeling of being away from everyone, lifted up on high.'

Given different circumstances, Ellen could have got on extremely well with this woman, but she felt more depressed now than she had done since being at Herbert's tea party.

The woman wanted to know what the neighbours were like. She put Daniel down on the floor to give her arms a rest.

'Not bad, most of them. Though the boy along the landing's kind of odd.' Odd? Yes, said Ellen, he had a habit of spying behind the peep-hole on the door and he could be a little sadistic, especially towards younger children. The woman's smile faded and she looked protectively down at Daniel who was trying to chew through a chair leg. 'And then there's Old Granny Morrison downstairs. Some of the kids say she's a witch.' Ellen laughed. 'You know what kids are like! She's just got a filthy temper and likes to scream a lot. But the rest of the neighbours are all right, more or less,' she finished up.

Oh well! The woman was stuck for words. She picked up Daniel and said she would need to be off, she'd think things over and if she was interested come back another time.

So that was that. The first hurdle was safely over and now they had the evening callers ahead.

It was fortunate that Davie's mother was going visiting at the hospital that evening and his father was taking the opportunity to go to the pub. That left the coast clear on the Dunlops' front. They had decided that all their activities would have to be limited to the stretch of stair after the bend coming up from the landing below so that they would not be observed by the second floor people who included Granny Morrison.

A few minutes before seven Ellen said that she was going out. Her mother, who was restlessly fidgeting from room to room picking up pieces of thread from the carpet and straightening mirrors, was just as pleased that she should absent herself.

She wanted the whole atmosphere to be one of desirability.

Ellen scuttled along the landing into Davie's flat. He had their props hidden in a cupboard in his bedroom: a bag of ashes, several crisp wrappers, orange peel going mouldy, a black banana skin, and a postcard on which were printed seven names.

'I'll take the ashes,' he said. 'In case you tip them on the floor before we get there.'

As he carried the bag, wisps of smoky grey wafted upward making him sneeze. Ellen stood back until he had got clear of the door and then she brought along the rest of the litter. On the top of the stair Davie paused; he opened the neck of the bag and flung the contents out. Choking and spluttering he retreated backwards into Ellen, making her shriek as he stepped on her foot.

'Shush, Ellie, for heaven's sake!'

They glanced at the Fergusons' door. It remained stolidly shut.

The ashes had certainly made enough mess, all over the banisters, as well as the steps themselves. Ellen quickly strewed the crisp wrappers, banana peel and orange skins, quite enjoying making patterns until Davie exhorted her to hurry and stop dithering. He was pinning the postcard on his own door. Ellen came up to read it.

> 'D. Ravioli
>
> Z. O. Van der Moos
>
> I. Gandhi
>
> J. Carter
>
> D. MacWheeble
>
> P. P. Zoblovnsky
>
> E. R. de Pompadour'

Ellen began to laugh.

'Shush, Ellie!'

'May I have this dance, Mr Ravioli?'

Davie grinned. 'Pleasure, Madame de Pompadour!' He held out his hands and they waltzed up the landing.

'Do you come here often?'

'Hey, there's someone coming.'

They peered down into the well of the stair and saw the bobbing heads of two people coming upward, a man's and a woman's. They were unknown heads.

'Quick!' cried Davie. 'Into the house!'

He shut the door behind them and Ellen stationed herself by the peep-hole, her eye as close to it as it would go.

The couple stopped. They must be reading the postcard, she felt sure they were. She could hear nothing except the strident din of the music behind her. And then she saw them move away. They were going towards the stairs, fast! She signalled to Davie to turn down the sound. She listened. Now she could hear their footsteps running on the stairs, *down* the stairs! She opened the door. Yes, they were running, and the landing was empty. They waited. The bottom door closed with a bang.

'Mr Ravioli, you're a marvel!'

Four couples came up as far as the Dunlops' door that evening.

At five minutes to eight Mrs Dunlop was observed entering the stair. In a panic they flew for brushes and shovels and were still clearing up when she arrived on the second landing.

'I dropped some rubbish, Mrs Dunlop,' said Ellen, most apologetic. 'But we're cleaning it up.' She gave her what she hoped was a melting smile. Mrs Dunlop was not known for her melting qualities except when folk were ill and then she was the first to appear at the door with a bowl of broth and her medicine kit.

'I can't think why I didn't get one single viewer,' said Mrs Ferguson, shaking her head over a bedtime cup of tea. 'Still, these things sometimes take a while.'

'You can't expect to sell the first day,' said Ellen.

'It's going to be an exhausting business keeping it up,' she said in the morning to Davie and Isadora on the way to school.

'We'll have to keep it up,' said Davie. 'Or else.'

'You can help tonight, Issie. You don't need to go out with Georgie Porgie every night.'

'You go and see your mysterious friend every day, don't you? What's his name, El? Come on, tell us! I'll give you half my Mars bar if you do.'

Ellen eyed it. 'OK, Nick.'

'Nick? Sounds like the devil.'

Ellen held out her hand for half the chocolate bar.

As the days and visiting hours went by she found she was getting quite expert at saying the right thing — or to be accurate, the wrong thing — to prospective purchasers. When they first stepped into the hall she tried to sum them up, to decide what their worst fears might be. If they had children then it was easy for there was the boy ogre on the landing, the witch below, the perils of the stairs themselves to work on. She built up a whole history of accidents that had taken place over the years and went from strength to strength elaborating on them. Everybody was worried about something and some were even stupid enough to ask if Ellen had enjoyed living here. The afternoons were not too bad but the evening sessions were something of a strain for then they had to be on their toes and it was not every evening that Mrs Dunlop went hospital visiting. Sometimes they only managed to put out the crisp bags and pin up the postcard but after the first three days the number of people coming up the stairs dropped off anyway. One or two did go past and ring the Fergusons' bell but Davie was not too downhearted. He said one must expect that, but at least they had greatly lowered the chances of the sale. Whenever someone did go in, they immediately went down into the street and began to make as much racket as they could and when the people came out they stepped it up and bounced the football against the door and wall.

By the end of the first week Old Granny Morrison

was not the only one who was complaining about the noise in the street.

They had one particularly hectic session in which they got the ashes splattered all over the second landing and were in the middle of sweeping them up when a viewer appeared behind them. He must have come up the stairs on rubber soles, walking on the balls of his feet like a burglar. 'Is this the stair where the flat's for sale?' he asked. 'It's been sold,' Ellen replied very fast, and he turned and went back down again.

At eight o'clock they went to the café and joined Isadora and George. Ellen let her elbows slump on to the table. She felt exhausted. It must be the nervous strain, she decided. They sat for almost two hours before heading home.

Herbert was having a supper of cocoa and chocolate biscuits in the sitting room. He smiled at Ellen, as did her mother, who seemed in a very good mood. She had that hint of gaiety thing in her smile again. Ellen watched her with apprehension.

'Herbert's got a little present for you, dear.'

'A present?'

He put his hand into his pocket and brought out a long oblong box which he passed to Ellen. She opened the lid and saw inside, lying in a bed of tissue paper, two strings of yellowed pearls. She stared at them.

'Lift them out then so that we can see,' said Mrs Ferguson.

Ellen lifted them up: the strands were attached to make a double string.

'What beautiful pearls, Herbert,' said Mrs Ferguson.

'My mother only went in for the best stuff.'

'Your mother?' Ellen looked at him.

'They were hers. She got them for her twenty-first.'

The pearls slipped through Ellen's fingers on to the floor.

'Ellen!' Mrs Ferguson gave a little scream and

dropped to her knees to retrieve them. She dusted them off gently. 'Let's try them on you, shall we?'

Ellen bent her head and her mother fixed the clasp.

'There now! They'll look better on the right dress of course. Go and look in the mirror.'

Ellen went and looked in the mirror above the mantelpiece and saw the two strings of yellow pearls lying against her emerald green T-shirt which had I AM A TEENAGE MONSTER printed across it in scarlet. The texture of the pearls reminded her of old teeth. Dead jewels!

'They suit you, Ellen,' said Herbert. 'I'm sure Mother would have wanted you to have them.

'What do you say to Herbert then, dear?'

'Thank you.'

'They're a sort of wedding present for you,' said Herbert. He sounded shy.

'Wedding present?'

'We hope to be married very soon.' He cleared his throat. 'And now I must be off, Rose. Work in the morning, eh?'

Ellen leant against the cool marble mantelpiece waiting whilst her mother saw Herbert out.

Mrs Ferguson re-entered the room briskly. 'Well now!' She began to plump a cushion.

'Mum, have you fixed the *day*?'

'A week on Saturday.'

'But I thought you were going to wait—'

'Now don't take on too much, love – but the flat is sold. The lawyer received an offer this morning and I accepted.'

SIX

The wedding took place at the local registry office at ten o'clock on the Saturday morning appointed. Mavis and an Insurance friend of Herbert's were the witnesses. Also present were Netta and Olive and of course Ellen, though there was, in fact, nothing inevitable about her presence for she had considered not coming. For several days she had maintained that she would stay away, that she detested Herbert, and his bungalow, and his mother's pearls. In the end she had capitulated, worn down, as she told Davie and Isadora, by the reproach in her mother's eyes, not to mention her tears. What did it matter anyway, one way or another? Their flat was sold. Their *home*. It had been bought by the cheerful woman with the baby Daniel She had come back about nine o'clock one evening and asked Mrs Ferguson if she could have another look, she had liked it so much. Apparently she had had some strange reservations about the neighbours but Mrs Ferguson had been able to reassure her and told her how kind Mrs Dunlop was, an ever-present help in times of trouble, and what a delightful boy Davie was, and that old Mrs Morrison's bark was much worse than her bite. She was quite a character, but what would the world be without characters?

The last two weeks had been a kind of nightmare and every morning on waking Ellen had hoped to find it had vanished with sleep. All she wanted was to be able to stay in her own home. It didn't seem much to ask. She was far too unadventurous, her mother told her, a real stick-in-the-mud. It was ridiculous at her age! She was tired of hearing about her age. Her mother moved through the flat with annoying cheerfulness and determination, throwing out the accumulated treasures of years. It was rubbish, said Mrs Ferguson. Ellen was a hoarder, her mother a discarder. Herbert's bungalow was not big enough to take all of Ellen's junk, not even her piano. It was when Mrs Ferguson announced that the piano could not come that the worst row erupted. She was sympathetic, she said, but Ellen must be reasonable, she would have to see that the piano just would not fit into the small bedroom at Herbert's. It was a physical impossibility. The room was only nine feet by seven and it already contained a bed, wardrobe, chest of drawers and a chair.

'Throw out the wardrobe and the chest of drawers.'

'Out of the question! Anyway, where would you put your clothes?'

'On the floor. The piano goes or I don't,' said Ellen.

The piano went to the Dunlops' and was put in Davie's room. Ellen could come in and play any time she wanted, said Mrs Dunlop. 'I think it's a crying shame you can't take your dad's piano with you, really I do.'

For Ellen that decided the matter: she would definitely not be going to go to live at Herbert's now. What would she do? asked Isadora. She would decide that during the next week whilst she was staying at Isadora's. Her mother and Herbert were going to Arran for the week on their honeymoon.

As they emerged from the registry office after the wedding, a photographer, festooned with cameras and light meters slung about his neck, jumped out of a parked car. He would take the happy couple on their own first, he announced. Ellen stood willingly aside. Turning her head she saw, on the opposite pavement, Isadora and Davie, who were watching the proceedings with looks of amazement on their faces. Somehow, they had talked about it so much that none of them had expected it to come off. But there was Mrs Ferguson, now Mrs Hall, in a froth of pink, holding the arm of Herbert who was decked out in a new navy-blue suit with a white carnation in his button-hole. The bride and groom.

'Smile please, watch the birdie! Say cheese!' Click, click, went the camera. The photographer glanced up and down the pavement.

Ellen glowered at Davie and Isadora defying them to wave to her. She felt the pearls weighing against her chest like stones. Her mother had insisted that she wear them and told her they looked marvellous on her new dress. The dress was the only thing that Ellen liked about the day; it was full-length and dark green, patterned with a small granny print.

'Your mother looks really lovely, Ellen.' Mavis sighed. 'Like a girl again.'

The photographer was signalling: he wanted the whole group now.

'Come on, Ellen,' said Mavis.

They had to wait for Ellen to get into line.

'Come on, dear,' said the photographer to Ellen. 'Smile! It's not a funeral you're at!'

Click, click, went the camera. The photographer winked at Ellen.

'Poor Ellie,' said Isadora on the opposite pavement.

For the final photograph the man decided it would be nice to have the bride and groom and the bride's daughter.

'Stand in closer, dear,' said Mrs Ferguson, now Mrs Hall, linking her arm through Ellen's.

Ellen kept her feet planted where they were but leaned slightly sideways to comply with her mother's request. The photographer pleaded with her to smile once more, repeating his funeral remark. She grim-aced and was snapped thus for posterity, to stand on Herbert's sideboard alongside his mother. She too had been wearing the double string of pearls to have her photograph taken.

They went back to Mavis's for drinks before having lunch at a small, French, cellar restaurant. The restaurant had been chosen by the bride who had had a word with the management beforehand to make sure that Herbert could have a steak well frazzled and untouched by any garlicked hand. Ellen sat between Herbert and his Insurance friend who, after two glasses of red wine, began to address the waiter in his own personal-type French which Ellen reproduced later for the benefit of Isadora and Davie. *Avez-vous?* he kept asking, putting great stress on the final letters of each word. After she herself had drunk two glasses of wine she began to giggle and then to hiccup and even to engage Herbert's friend in excrutiating French conversation.

'Sounds like a drunken orgy,' said Isadora. They were sitting in the café drinking coke, the happy couple having set off from Waverley Station for Arran an hour before.

'At least the food was yummy,' said Ellen. She had not expected to eat a bite but once the smells assailed her, her appetite had returned.

'You never think of anything but your stomach!'

There was an obvious retort to make to Isadora in return and Ellen made it. Ever since they had come in to the café, Isadora had been watching a boy who was sitting a couple of tables away and he had been watching her. She had broken with George the night before, over his homework.

'Who is that, Davie? Do you know him?'

Davie shrugged. He thought his name was Tony, but no, he was not going to go over and speak to him and drag him across to be introduced to Isadora! She could do her own dirty work.

'All right! No need to be such a nark!' She propped her chin on her hand. 'Tony's a nice name, don't you think?'

'Oh no Antonio!' sang Ellen, upsetting Isadora's state of dreaminess. Ellen was the absolute end to have as a friend, she declared, and could be relied upon to give you a red face in any situation. She tossed her silky blonde hair and got up to put another coin in the juke box taking care to pass close to Tony's table as she went.

'Let's go for a walk, Davie,' said Ellen. 'I'm restless.' She got to her feet and called out, 'See you later, Issie.'

Issie was too preoccupied with the juke box to answer. She seemed to be having trouble in getting her money in the slot. Ellen and Davie did not wait to see Tony get up and go to her aid.

'Oh no Antonio,' sang Ellen, as they walked along by the Water of Leith, taking the path that ran westward from Stockbridge to the Dean Village. The sun shone with mid-afternoon brightness making the water sparkle and the green leaves glitter. The noise of the city above came to them remotely, the vague hum of traffic seeming to intensify the feeling of peace down by the water. Some boys were hanging over the fence fishing. They themselves had often fished here and once Davie had caught a minnow.

By St Bernard's Well they paused a while. It was one of Ellen's favourite spots. Every time she came upon it, it was with some feeling of surprise for it looked like a miniature Greek temple. Between the columns was a statue of Hygeia, goddess of health, and down below, inside the building, was the spring whose waters people used to come and drink for the sake of their health in days gone by. Hygeia stood, her noble back to the river, her smooth face to the sun, serenely holding a drinking vessel in her right hand.

Ellen and Davie went down on to the wooden-floored balcony behind the temple and leant on the railing to watch the rather murky river flow past below. 'It's a wonder that they didn't all drop dead immediately,' said Ellen. 'The spring must have come out of *that*.' Her affection for the river would not extend to drinking it.

After a while they moved to a park bench beside the well where they too could turn their faces to the sun, like Hygeia. Davie produced two apples. He was like a magician, said Ellen: he always had something concealed on his person somewhere.

'D'you know something, Davie? I think I shall take up residence here, with Hygeia. I've always fancied living in a temple. I could open up the well again and dish out the waters.'

The sound of the water flowing ceaselessly behind them and the warmth of the sun smoothed away her restlessness. It did seem possible to stay here for ever. They sat until the sun moved round in the sky and began to lower. Isadora's mother would be wondering where Ellen was, said Davie, she would be cooking up her brown rice and black-eyed beans and pouring out the buttermilk.

She was standing on her head in the hall when Isadora and Ellen let themselves in. Isadora had been tapping her foot at the end of the street when Ellen returned with Davie. She had just bought herself an 'afternoon dress' in pearl grey crêpe de Chine from a shop in St Stephen Street and was dying to show it to Ellen. It was a dress in which one might have gone to a tea dance. 'You know the kind of thing, with palm court orchestras and all of that.' They had read about them and Isadora regretted they were no longer a part of modern life. Ellen had never been able to imagine herself at such an affair until now, when she did, with Nick. They glided between the palms (there must be palms), the black-suited orchestra players playing Strauss waltzes.

'Hello there, Ellie,' said Mrs MacBain, upside down. Isadora was holding the bag containing the afternoon dress behind her back. Her mother said she threw her money down the drain. 'How did it go?' Ellen looked blank: Nick's arms were round her waist and the musicians were smiling at them. 'The wedding!'

Oh, the wedding! Between Rose Elizabeth Ferguson

and Herbert Hall. Ellen did not know whether to turn her head upside down or not to answer, so compromised by putting it sideways. Mrs MacBain began to lower her feet slowly until they touched the floor, then she sprang upright to face them. She was wearing a royal blue leotard.

'You girls need to take up yoga. Look at you, Isadora! Slouching like an old woman. Stand up as if you were proud of your body!'

They had nut casserole for dinner and Mr MacBain had a lamb chop.

'I wouldn't eat any of yon muck if you paid me. What do you think of it, eh, Ellie? Bet you'd rather have had a good fat chop.'

Ellen was fiddling about with the food on her plate not because she objected to it being vegetarian – she did not really mind that – but because she had no appetite. For once. There was a queasiness in the pit of her stomach that had nothing to do with food and whenever she thought of their old flat lying up there stripped bare of all their possessions the unsettled feeling quickened into pain. Mrs MacBain was eyeing her with an expression that said 'Yoga!' Perhaps standing on one's head might not be such a bad idea: it might stop one thinking.

'Don't be encouraging the girls to adopt your impure tastes, Tom,' said Mrs MacBain. 'Chops will do nothing for them.' Six months before she had been eating meat herself and no one doubted that in six months' time when she had found a new enthusiasm to preoccupy her, she would be eating it again. As Isadora said, it was best to humour her and not worth arguing. Only her husband argued which he did good humouredly. The only time he was to be seen in a bad mood was when Isadora did not come home on time. That sent his blood pressure soaring.

'You'll be going out with Ellie tonight then, Isadora?' he said before leaving the table.

'Oh yes,' said Isadora, violet-blue eyes opened wide.

'We're meeting Tony at half-seven,' she whispered as soon as the door closed on her mother and father.

'*We* are?'

'Yes. I told him all about you. He doesn't mind you coming.'

'Thanks very much. For nothing! You can go on your own, Isadora MacBain!'

'Oh, come on now, Ellie.'

Isadora wheedled Ellen over the washing-up offering bribes, all of which were rejected.

'You don't have to worry about me,' said Ellen loftily, when they had put all the dishes away, deciding that it was time to relieve Isadora of her misery. 'I have a date of my own this evening.'

'With Nick? You are a close one! What's he like, Ellie, apart from being tall, dark and handsome?'

Ellen considered, looking into the mid-distance, smiling a little. He was very interesting and a lot of fun and kind and – well, what else could one say? She shrugged. 'He's just fantastic! We have so much in common.'

'What, for example?' demanded Isadora.

'Music.'

'Does he play the piano?'

Ellen nodded. 'He certainly does! He could become a concert pianist. Or a jazz musician.'

Isadora was much impressed. She tried to find out now where Ellen had met him but should have known better than to ask, for Ellen merely smiled more maddeningly than ever.

'What age is he?'

'Eighteen going on nineteen.'

'Eighteen!'

They walked along the street together and Isadora's mind seemed more preoccupied with Nick than Tony who after all was only fifteen and a half and had pimples on the back of his neck.

'Where are you meeting him? All right, sorry I asked! But I think you're really mean, I tell you everything. . . .' Isadora chuntered on until halted by the approach of Tony. She introduced him and Ellen, and they stood for a few minutes talking on the corner.

'What do you have in mind for us to do this evening, Tony?' asked Isadora.

'Fancy going for a coke?'

'I thought we might make up a foursome with Ellen and her boyfriend.'

'Sorry,' said Ellen, 'but we have other plans. We're going gambling at the casino.'

With that she left them and hurried to Nicolas's, looking back to check every few yards, knowing Isadora as she did.

Nicolas was sitting by his window waiting for her.

'Did you ever play roulette, Nicolas?' she asked.

He had, when he was much younger, had even been to the casino in Monte Carlo.

'Really? Tell me about it! Please!'

She loved him to tell her about the things he used to do. He told her about Monte Carlo and the Riviera, he reminisced about Paris and then about Czechoslovakia, going back to the days of his youth, to when he was Ellen's age. It all sounded so much more interesting and romantic than her life in Edinburgh that she began to think she had been born in the wrong country at the wrong time. Nicolas laughed. Every age, every country, had it drawbacks, *and* its attractions.

'You don't think so, Ellen! But you have a lot of freedom, much more than I had as a boy.'

She sighed. Freedom meant the street, their flat, their old life; she could not associate it with Herbert, his bungalow, that south-side suburb. She must keep an open mind, cautioned Nicolas: to have a closed one was one of the worst sins as far as he was concerned.

'You miss too much that way!'

He got up to play for her; she was not in a mood to play herself. She felt strangely tired even though she had done no work of any kind that day. A lassitude enveloped her body as she lay back on the veloured sofa listening to the music flowing and rippling round her. She could almost have slept. The last of the evening sun had turned to a mellow gold and was lighting up the wall behind the piano, touching the top of Nicolas's white head and his long sensitive hands. A sigh of peace escaped her. She so loved this room with its paintings and books and plants: it soothed and relaxed her and erased all thoughts of Herbert. She had taken off the pearls but still wore the long dark green dress. It smelled of fresh cotton and made her feel a quite different person, not like Ellie Ferguson any more. In it she felt she could float and dance and dream.

'Are you asleep, Ellen?'

She blinked. The music had stopped and Nicolas was standing over her. His eyes seemed more blind than ever.

'Are your eyes worse, Nicolas?'

He nodded. 'The cataracts have crossed.'

She sat up.

'I go into hospital on Monday, Ellen.'

She wanted to cry out 'No!' when she should be glad that his long wait would soon be over. But things would never be the same for them again. She said nothing.

'I'll still need your help when I come home, you know.'

'For a while. Oh, I'm sorry! How selfish I am! I was thinking about *me*, when I should have been thinking about you. Isn't that terrible?'

He would not agree since he considered that it was only natural. But things would be the same, he said. She could come and cook for him, if she was still willing, and he would give her music lessons, the only difference being that he would be able to see her properly and not just as a blur. She said that was no advantage and he laughed, and then so did she.

81

'Life never can stay exactly the same, Ellen. It would be a mistake to expect it to. Anyway, I want to see you!'

Could she come in each day while he was away and practise on the piano? She would look after the flat too and give it a spring-clean. He protested but she said that she would love to, she would have nothing much to do all week whilst she was staying at the MacBains, for Isadora would be out with Tony and she did not want to have to tag behind playing gooseberry. All right! He accepted saying that he would be happy to know she would be coming in every day and playing on his piano.

She came back to visit him on Sunday and found Mavis there feeding him with walnut cake. Mavis was full of praises for the wedding; she enthused over the bride's dress and her hair and the lovely lunch and the happiness of the happy couple. Ellen wanted to scream but, looking at Nicolas's calm, composed face, refrained. Could she ever be so serene? Mavis did not go. She seemed settled in for the afternoon and in the end Ellen had to leave first as Isadora's mother was having people to tea and wanted the girls to help her.

She hesitated in the doorway. 'Good luck. Can I come to visit you?'

'Of course.'

Mavis said that she would tell Ellen which ward Nicolas would be in and when she could visit him.

The operation took place on Tuesday. All day in school Ellen kept thinking about it and wondering how Nicolas was getting on. What if he were to die? He had said the operation was a comparatively safe one but anything could happen, he was an old man, his heart might give out. . . .

She had to ask permission to leave the room so that she could go and be sick in the cloakroom. Isadora was sent after her.

'Are you all right, Ellie? Gosh, what a colour your

face is!' Isadora went for the nurse who laid Ellen out on the couch in the medical room for the rest of the morning and covered her with a tartan blanket. Ellen lay and looked at the ceiling until eventually her eyelids could not stay open any longer and she slept. When the nurse came back she made some stupid remark about her outgrowing her own strength and then released her.

What about a game of football after he'd done his paper round in the afternoon? suggested Davie; that would bring the colour back to her cheeks. If she liked she could even help him with the papers, which she did, wanting to fill the time till she could go and ask Mavis for news. Mavis did not come home from work till six.

They collected a number of kids in the street once they began to play and Ellen entered into the game with even more determination and concentration than usual. She needed to run with all the strength in her legs, kick the ball with all her might, yell with all the wind in her lungs.

'Davie! Hey, Dunlop, come on, come on!'

The ball came sizzling down the street, bounced at an angle against the roof of a parked car and went sideways into an open stair.

'Clever clogs!' shouted Ellen.

Granny Morrison's window went up with a rattle and her head came out. 'Oh, it's you, Ellie Ferguson!'

Ellen looked up. 'Yes, it's me, Mrs Morrison.'

'I thought you didn't live in our street any more.'

Ellen turned and walked quickly down the street. Davie came after her catching her up just around the corner.

'Don't be silly, Ellie! It's only Old Granny Morrison. She doesn't count.'

'She's right — I don't live there in the street any more. I don't live anywhere.'

'You can always come to the street, you know you can.'

'I don't. I don't know any such thing.'

'But you're staying at Issie's anyway just now.'

'As a visitor.'

She was going for a walk now, she said, and wanted to go alone. He let her go.

She walked down by the temple of Hygeia and sat beside the river bank until she heard six strike. She met Mavis as she was coming along her street on her way home from work. She was smiling. Nicolas was fine, he had come through the operation very well and Ellen could go to see him the next day.

She visited him every afternoon and spent as much time as she could get away from Isadora in the evenings in his flat. She played the piano but sometimes just sat looking around the room imagining that she lived here. How she would love to! Perhaps she could come and be a kind of au pair to Nicolas when he came back from hospital. If Nicolas was to speak to her mother. . . . The idea ran out at the thought of her mother. She and Herbert were having a lovely time in Arran, she had written on a postcard; the island was beautiful and they had climbed Goat Fell, its highest mountain, and bathed in the sea. 'We must bring you here sometime, dear,' she had concluded.

Ellen went over to the shelf where Nicolas's photographs stood and picked up the one of the dark young man leaning against a wall in Paris. She stared into his face. She liked his eyes and his laughter. His laughter was easy to imagine. 'May I have the pleasure of this dance, Nick?' She began to waltz, round and round the room, humming *The Blue Danube,* holding Nick between the palms of her hands. Whilst they danced they smiled at one another. Perhaps Nick would come to Edinburgh in time for the end of the year school dance and he would be her partner and she would be the belle of the ball in her long green dress! She twirled faster and faster until she came to rest against the window, laughing.

The door opened behind her.

'Oh, it's you, Ellen,' said Mavis. 'I wondered who was moving about overhead.'

Quickly Ellen hid the photograph behind her back. She said that she was just about to go. She took Nick with her.

'Where *do* you get to all the time?' grumbled Isadora as they were getting ready for bed. Preparing for bed was for her a major operation: clothes must be selected, tried, if necessary discarded, and others chosen. Tonight she wore pink silk cami-knickers, an oyster-coloured satin nightdress with lace trimming, and a blue and gold silk kimono. Since her mother would not let her cross the doorstep in any of the clothes she bought in the second-hand shops (she would slave to buy them, baby-sitting, shopping, even stair-washing) her only option was to get as much wear out of them as she could inside the house. If only her mother would be a bit more open-minded then she could easily have worn the oyster-coloured nightie as a dress. Her room smelt of old clothes, mothballs, and camphor. When she went to school in the morning, her mother came in and pushed the window up high and when Isadora came home in the afternoon she shut it down tight. Now she was smearing liquid paraffin over her face, a practice they had seen recommended in a Sunday Colour Supplement. 'Ellie, why can't I get to meet him? Are you hiding some dark secret from me? Is he married or something?'

'Married?' Ellen began to laugh and the bed to shake. She laughed and laughed until Isadora told her to hush, for goodness' sake, or her mother would be in imagining that Ellen was having hysterics and then she might start to advocate herbal potions or the triangular pose. She had said that afternoon that she thought Ellen was a bit disturbed at present and Isadora must be careful and considerate with her. 'Nick married? He's only eighteen.'

Some people were married at seventeen, even

sixteen, said Isadora. In Scotland that was the age of consent after all.

'Well, Nick is not. Issie, would you like to see a picture of him?'

She allowed Isadora to take the photograph into her own hand. For a minute Isadora did not speak.

'But he's beautiful, Ellie,' she said at last. She seemed stunned.

Ellen smiled, held out her hand to take Nick back. She slept that night with him on the table beside her bed and when she wakened in the morning she found herself looking into his smiling eyes.

'Good morning, Nick,' she said softly.

'I really would love to meet him, El.'

'I might bring him to the school dance.'

'You must!'

That afternoon in the hospital she asked Nicolas if he would like her to write to any of his relatives in Paris to let them know about his operation. She would write reassuringly and be careful not to say anything that would worry them. 'I could write to your nephew if you like,' she said diffidently.

'That's a splendid idea,' said Nicolas. Did he smile? She was not sure. But he went on to say that he had wanted to communicate with Nick again and not been able to write for some time because of his failing sight. And she could write in English for although Nick could not speak it all that well he could certainly read it.

She wrote from Nicolas's flat, putting that address at the top. 'My name is Ellen Rose Ferguson (the Rose added interest, she decided). I am almost fifteen years old (she had only ten months to go, after all)'. She paused, reread the sentence. Then she tore the paper up. How ridiculous! It sounded like she was writing to him as a pen friend. She began again: 'I am a friend of your uncle Nicolas's.' But he might think she was a friend of Mavis's age. 'I am a young friend of your uncle Nicholas's.' That was better. She read the

86

sentence several times over, chewed her pen, scratched her head with it. 'He has just had an operation on his eyes but you must not be alarmed.' She found that her language came stiltedly for she could not rid her mind of the knowledge that Nick was French and she could not therefore write to him as she would have done to Davie.

The letter took two hours to write. She dropped it into a pillar box on the way home and imagined his dark eyes reading it in Paris. He might lean against that wall to read it. The next day she wrote another one to keep him informed on his uncle's progress and in this letter allowed herself to mention that she played the piano and Nicolas was her teacher.

Each night she slept with the photograph propped up beside her bed. Isadora eyed her with wonder.

'You know, Ellie, I never thought that you—'

'What?'

'Oh nothing.'

The week was going on.

Ellen wrote again to Nick telling him that his uncle's bandages were being removed and that she was reading *Scarlet and Black* by Stendahl aloud to him. 'I am fond of Stendahl,' she wrote. 'Are you? I like *Madame Bovary* also.' She had seen it dramatised on television. Was it by Stendahl or Flaubert? Never mind! At least it was French and she had enjoyed it. Before Nick came to Edinburgh she would read the book and they would be able to discuss it together intelligently.

'Your mum'll be back tomorrow, Ellie,' said Mrs MacBain at breakfast, jolting Ellen, who had not realised that Friday had come already.

Tomorrow her mother would be back with Herbert.

SEVEN

'Arran was simply beautiful,' said Mrs Hall.

'I know,' said Ellen. 'You've said so already.'

But her mother was not listening. She was sighing for the delights of Arran and gazing fondly at Herbert.

'You'd like it, Ellen. It's got everything: mountains, sea, rivers, everything in miniature.'

'We could take a caravan for a week in August, Rose.'

'What a marvellous idea, Herbert! Wouldn't that be nice, Ellen?'

'We always used to go to France, when Dad was alive. Remember?'

'We went once, dear.'

'I can remember—'

'Only once. To Brittany.'

'We camped. It was fantastic fun.'

'It rained the whole time.'

'I remember the sun shining.'

'The rain never let up. We came home a week early.'

'That's not true!'

'I'm afraid it is, dear. Your father couldn't stand being cooped up in a small tent, he was a fair weather man, all right as long as things were going well.'

Herbert had been clearing his throat and shuffling his feet for the past few minutes, now he stood up and announced that he thought he would take a wee turn around the garden to see how the roses were doing.

'If you take two turns you'll end up in the street,' said Ellen.

He frowned, not comprehending. He was a man on whom sarcasm was wasted, Ellen was quickly finding out.

'Why don't you, dear?' put in his wife quickly. 'The air'll do you good.' When he had gone she turned on Ellen. 'How dare you speak to Herbert like that? He's giving you a good home.'

'I already had one.'

'Why do you have to be so unpleasant? I know it's difficult for you but you have got to try! Do you know your trouble, Ellen? You only see what you want to see.'

Ellen got up and went to perch on the narrow window sill. Not that there was anything to see in the street. There seldom was. At least half the people had retired and the other half ought to. The biggest event was the arrival of the milkman clanking his bottles at seven in the morning and the postman whistling at eight. She reckoned he needed to whistle to keep his spirits up. On Sunday Herbert had had a sherry party for the neighbours, the men had worn grey office suits and the women crimplene dresses encrusted with diamante clips, and the first question everyone had asked was what school was she at. Her mother, with a little tinkly laugh, had said, 'The eternal Edinburgh question!' causing Ellen to stare at her in surprise for it had never been any kind of question in their flat or Isadora's or Davie's. They had all gone automatically to their local school. What the people were asking was did she go to a fee-paying school. Afterwards her mother had broached the matter with Herbert asking him what he thought, should they perhaps try to make the sacrifice for Ellen, it might be the making of her? Ellen hearing the conversation through the wall – it being impossible not to – rushed through to say she didn't want to go to any school other that the one she was at. There was no need for any sacrifices. Her mother was not finished yet though for if Ellen did not fancy a fee-paying school why should she not transfer to the state school for this area? There were two nice girls round the corner who went there, Ellen might become friends with them, and she would be saved all that travelling.

'You can't expect me to give up everything!'

'Leave it, Rose.' Herbert had had the last word.

But the next day her mother had invited the two nice girls to tea. She made an especially attractive meal of chicken and salad, baked a chocolate and walnut cake, and put a bowl of red roses in the middle of the table. 'It's far too fussy,' said Ellen, who refused to change out of her jeans into her green dress. The girls turned up in dresses and brought a box of chocolate mints for Mrs Hall. She was thrilled with both the mints and the girls. She talked to them non-stop whilst Ellen ate. 'You didn't even try,' her mother said when they had gone home after thanking her for a lovely tea. 'Try for what?' Ellen wanted to know. She didn't need friends, she had Davie and Isadora, as well as all the other girls at school. Friends often change with circumstances, said her mother, horrifying Ellen.

'You won't drop Mavis and Netta and Olive now, will you?'

'Of course not. Though I don't suppose I shall see them as often. Be sensible! How could I, now that I have Herbert?'

Herbert was taking several turns around the garden.

'Ellen, is it such a dreadful idea to consider changing schools? Some children change cities.'

'They don't usually have to change fathers at the same time.'

'You didn't have a father.' There was silence for a moment between them before her mother went on, 'I'm sorry to have to say that, dear, but it does happen to be true and I think it's time you faced up to reality. You spend far too much time in a dream world.'

'You'll end up as bad as Herbert. He doesn't like dreaming!'

'There are dreams and dreams. You can't go on—'
She broke off and sighed.

'You hated my father, didn't you?'

'No, I wouldn't say that, Ellen. But I wasn't very happy with him.'

'Well, I was. And don't tell me I don't remember for I do!'

'All right I won't. Are you so unhappy here, love?'

'Yes, I am! What is there for me to do out here?' Ellen cried.

'You could read, practise your 'cello, join the local tennis club.'

There was nothing to be said in answer to that. Ellen stared at Herbert's mother. 'I feel she's watching me all the time. Her eyes move.'

Sharply, her mother reproved her, telling her not to talk such rubbish. Her patience, which was not superabundant at any time (a fact she admitted herself), was evaporating. Herbert said that she should just leave Ellen to come round in her own way but this was not as easy for her to do as for him to say. Ellen lay around the sitting room, her arms and legs spread as far as she could fling them, yawning openly and untiringly. Or else she did not come home at all. Sometimes she went out to school at eight o'clock in the morning and did not return till ten at night. She said she had been working for her old man who was recovering from his operation, she had promised to spring-clean his flat. Her mother felt sure she had been hanging about in their old street.

Ellen wrinkled her nose at Herbert's mother. Every mealtime they heard about her culinary expertise, every evening about her goodness. She had never hated anyone as much in her life as she did this determined-looking woman with the double string of pearls about her throat. Beside her stood the picture of Ellen herself with the pearls and her mother and Herbert in their wedding outfits. She began to laugh.

'What is it, Ellen?'

'Look at my eyes in the photograph! They look as if they're scowling straight at Herbert's mother.' Ellen laughed until the tears came. Her mother got up and rearranged the photographs so that Ellen scowled instead at a group of china shepherdesses bedecked with rosebuds.

Now Ellen yawned, a deep, wide yawn, and stretched out her arms. One hand flicked the tail of a plaster duck where it flew across the wall, and set it into a tremble.

'Ellen, please!' Her mother pounced on the duck with both hands and held it fast.

'Sorry. But there just isn't room for me in this little house. I feel as if my arms and legs should stick out through the doors and windows. It was made for midgets.'

'I wish you would stop exaggerating.'

'Everything about this place gives me the shudders: the street, the neighbours, Herbert. . . .'

That would most certainly do! Her mother's temper rocketed. Ellen retreated to her bedroom but not before she had glanced through the window and noticed the two nice girls coming down the street towards Herbert's house. They looked purposeful as if they bore an invitation. She was escaping just in time. 'So, OK,' she said to her father's photograph, silently, since she could not speak to him aloud in this place, 'maybe I'm not acting what you'd call too grown up but you understand how I feel, don't you? You're the only one who does apart from Nicolas and even he says some things must be tolerated. But I *hate* Herbert!' She glanced around, guiltily almost, for she could hardly believe she had not spoken out loud.

The door opened, her mother looked in. She wore a placating smile. 'Now listen, dear,' she began. Ellen must be reasonable – the eternal cry! Wendy and Debbie had come to ask her to tea at their house this afternoon. Wasn't that nice of them? She wasn't four years old, said Ellen unwisely, giving her mother the

92

ammunition for a retort. It was terrible but since her mother's return from Arran everything had turned into a kind of battle between them. They had seldom fought in the old days.

Ellen said she had promised to visit Nicolas in hospital that afternoon. Visiting the sick was something to be commended and not an activity that could be criticised. Her mother sighed and went back to tell the girls that Ellen was terribly sorry, and perhaps another day?

In the narrow room Ellen stood stretching her arms as wide as they would go. She felt so cramped. Perhaps she was beginning to suffer from claustrophobia and if it were to be confirmed medically then they would have to let her move out of here to save her sanity. She lifted her anorak and opened the door.

Her mother and Herbert were talking in the sitting room.

'It'll work out all right in the end, Rose, you'll see. She must feel strange here. I must seem strange to her, after all. She'll settle down, given time.'

'I'm not so sure, Herbert. You see, she's awfully like her father.'

'Thank goodness for that,' said Ellen to a picture of Herbert's mother on the wall in the lobby. There were likenesses of the woman everywhere and in each of them she had that same penetrating stare that seemed to bore a hole in your head.

The sitting-room door opened and Herbert appeared in the doorway. 'Ellen!' He said her name with an air of helplessness. 'Is there anything I can do for you?'

'No thank you. I'm just going into town.'

She knew they would be watching from the window as she walked along the road. It was Sunday afternoon. Not a whisper disturbed the air. A terylene curtain twitched further up. She supposed they must have caused some ripples of interest. Fancy Herbert Hall getting married at last! What next? At breakfast that morning her mother had announced that Herbert was about to purchase a car expecting her to be excited by the prospect when she knew very well that the money for the car was coming from the sale of their flat. They were talking about buying a caravan as well and then all three of them could go touring Scotland together. They must be out of their minds!

Nicolas had just been moved to a convalescent hospital where he would spend a week or two and then, if all went well, he would be allowed home.

He was sitting beside his bed in his dressing-gown and he had a letter in his hand, one with a French stamp. He had had a nurse read it to him but Ellen should read it for herself and learn what news it contained.

The letter was in French and her comprehension of that language was a bit shaky but she knew enough to understand *'Je viendrai à Edimbourg.'*

'When?' she cried, scouring the lines for a date. 'When?' In just over two weeks' time!

'Isn't that nice? I am so looking forward to seeing him again.'

'And just think, Nicolas, you will be able to *see* him!'

They were deprived of the joy of discussing Nick's impending visit further by the arrival of Mavis. She came briskly up the ward laden with shopping baskets. Soon she was unpacking fresh eggs and raspberry jam and home-made queen cakes. Nicolas's bed began to resemble a cake and candy stall.

Mavis wanted to hear all about Ellen's mother and Herbert and how things were at the bungalow.

'A laugh a minute,' said Ellen.

That only drew a lecture from Mavis and a shake of the head from Nicolas. He kept telling her she had to be positive. The only times she felt positive were when she was playing the piano or talking to him. But talking to him with Mavis there could not be counted, for Mavis ran on about her cakes and then the plumber who took two days to come and unblock her sink and the grocer on the corner who ripped her off every time she went into his shop. They stayed until Nicolas's tea was brought round.

'Are you going to go and practise now, Ellen?' he asked. 'Make sure you don't neglect your scales. I shall be expecting great things when I come home.'

'If you're going to Nicolas's you can chum me home then, Ellen,' said Mavis.

Mavis came up into Nicolas's flat with her. She seemed to want company. She missed Ellen's mother, she said; they had been great pals and gone everywhere together. Oh, not that she grudged Rose her happiness, certainly not! One must take happiness in life when and where one found it.

By the shelf of photographs she paused. She frowned. 'Funny! Could have sworn there was another picture there. What was it of now?' She shrugged, unable to remember. 'He's a lovely man, Nicolas, isn't he?'

Warily, Ellen agreed. She watched Mavis covertly whilst she studied all the photographs which she must have looked at many times before. She was staring at one of Nicolas as a young man. Surely she would not think of marrying Nicolas or he her? Isadora had said jokingly one day, 'Mavis'll be next.' Whom did she have in mind? Ellen had wanted to know. Isadora was of the opinion that 'There must be some old geyser she could have.' Ellen took another look at Mavis's preoccupied expression and felt the sweat start around her hairline and on the palms of her hands. She was trembling too. Nothing was impossible, not now. She sat down and began to play the Chopin nocturne Nicolas had played to her the very first day she had come here. Mavis put down the photograph and came to the piano.

'I recognise that.'

Ellen nodded.

'You do play really well, Ellen, you know. Your

mother should never have tried to discourage you. I know she was badly hurt but still!' She shook her head and then went away. Ellen listened to her feet descending the stairs and the door of her flat closing beneath. Silence filled Nicolas's flat.

This was now the only place in which she felt at home. She knew, as Mrs MacBain and Mrs Dunlop told her, that she was welcome to come to both their houses at any time, but when she did and saw Isadora and Davie in their usual places it reminded her even more of her own old home. She had tried to play her dad's piano in Davie's room but that hadn't worked either. One day the cheerful woman who had bought their flat had passed her on the stair with baby Daniel on her hip and asked if she'd like to come up for a cup of coffee. She had hardly been able to get an answer out before running helter-skelter down the stairs into the street. When she was not in Nicolas's flat she spent hours along by the Water of Leith or sitting in the café with Isadora and her boyfriend who was now called Tom (Tom, Tom, the piper's son) or with Davie.

She sat in Nicolas's chair by the window and let the sun heat her face. She sat till the sun went down, then moved to the piano where she played for an hour or more. After that there was nothing to be done but make the long trek back out to Herbert's bungalow. She had been living there for two weeks. It felt like two years.

Sunday came again. Sundays were the worst days, by far. The street stirred as the church bells began to ring and a few people in Sunday coats and hats emerged from their bungalows, her mother and Herbert amongst them. Her mother hadn't been to church for years, Ellen remarked, a remark which was turned briskly aside. Her mother had always been too tired in the past to go to church, had needed a long lie in on a Sunday morning to get over Saturday in the shop but she had always wanted to go more often. She enjoyed going to Herbert's church: they met some very nice people there. It would do Ellen good to come with them instead of lying in her bed half the morning feeling sorry for herself.

'I do not feel sorry for myself,' she said, and after the door closed on her mother, muttered, 'I feel sorry for you.'

She lay in bed all morning playing music on her record player and did not hear her mother and Herbert coming back. Herbert surprised her by putting his head round the door. He seldom came into her room. He coughed, cleared his throat – she saw but did not hear – and looked embarrassed. She turned down the sound of the record player.

'That's better.' He cleared his throat again. 'Matter of fact, Ellen—' She looked at him; he continued. 'The people next door—' He did not go on, did not need to, for now she knew the cause of his embarrassment.

'Have they been complaining?'

He nodded. She turned the record player right off and slid down in bed pulling the covers over her head. She knew it was scarcely fair to take it out on Herbert but she wanted to for after all if he had never appeared on the scene – their scene – she wouldn't have to live in this claustrophobic house amongst all these claustrophobic people who couldn't stand any noise above a whisper and were on the watch all the time for anyone transgressing their unwritten rules. Her mother said she was becoming neurotic, imagining things, or inventing them, but she saw, even if her mother did not, the faces behind the curtains and the sly sideways looks cast in her direction. She did not belong here and they all knew it.

That week she stayed later and later on the other side of the town and each evening on returning she and her mother had a row.

'You can't go on like this, Ellen.'

'What else can I do?'

'Come home at the proper time.'

'Home?'

Then her mother would erupt but try to keep her voice at a carefully controlled level knowing that the wall between the houses was thin and the people on the other side seemed to have exceptionally sharp ears.

When Ellen lay in bed she heard her mother say to Herbert, 'This can't go on, Herbert,' and Herbert said, 'We must be patient, Rose.' After this exchange they both sighed. It would be better for them if she was out of the way; she was just a drag on their life together and did not see how she could ever be otherwise. She contemplated going to London but knew that contemplation was as far as it would go since she had just under four pounds in the post office savings bank and could imagine only too well the horrors of being alone and penniless in a big city. London didn't appeal to her much, except for a visit; all that she wanted was to go back to her father's flat.

'Not too much to ask for, is it?' she asked him.

He smiled back at her.

Obviously what she wanted was impossible so she would have to go for the next best thing and without any contemplation knew what that would be.

On Saturday she visited Nicolas, had lunch at Isadora's and went for a walk by the river in the afternoon with Davie.

'You're awful quiet today,' said Davie, as they sat by St Bernard's Well.

'I'm thinking.'

'What about?'

Ellen shrugged.

She went back to Herbert's early that evening.

'How nice!' cried her mother.'We were about to eat so you're just in time, dear.'

Her mother had made a lemon meringue pie, her first ever. The meringue had risen beautifully, was light and dry. Herbert praised it lavishly and his wife laughed, turning pink in the cheek and saying that she was sure it wouldn't have been a patch on his mother's.

'It's better,' he said, without even a glance at his mother's face. 'Oh, yes, definitely.'

The pink in Rose's cheek deepened. Ellen looked away.

Her own appetite was poor and her mother fussed making her feel a little guilty. But she had to push her guilt aside: her plan was laid. One must preserve one's sanity, or else one would go under. She had heard her mother say that many a time in the past. Survival comes first.

About nine o'clock she said that she thought she would have an early night. Was she feeling all right? asked her mother. Sore throat? Headache? She did look a bit pale and heavy under the eyes. She was just tired, she said.

Ellen got ready for bed and then pulled out her rucksack from the bottom of the cupboard. She listened. Her mother and Herbert were watching television and the sitting-room door was shut. She packed some clean underwear and socks, two T-shirts, a packet of biscuits and chocolate bought earlier in the day, two paperback books, her father's photographs and the one of Nick. She buckled up the straps and put the rucksack under the bed, then got under the covers.

They stayed up till the television closed down for the night. She lay in the dark listening to the rise and fall of the voices and the intermissions of music. Then silence descended. After a moment the sitting-room door opened and she heard her mother yawn. Herbert went to check the front and back doors, double-locking both against possible intruders. First her mother went to the bathroom and then Herbert and, finally, both retired. Ellen lay listening, fighting off waves of sleep that wanted to engulf her. They did.

She awoke with a start. Light was creeping in

between the gap in the curtains, a grey thin light which meant that dawn was breaking. She looked at her watch. Four-thirty. She would still be all right: they must be dead asleep at this time. Very quietly she got up pausing in alarm at the squeaking of the bed springs but heard no sound from anywhere except the cheepings of a bird in the garden. She pulled on her jeans and gym shoes, her anorak, and then took out the rucksack.

On the ledge in the hall below the portrait of Herbert's mother, she left her letter. She saluted Herbert's mother silently and the woman's eyes stared back without wavering. She was one person she would not miss.

It would be best to leave by the back door, she had decided: being better concealed, there would be less chance of detection by the neighbours. Not that people should be peeping behind their curtains at this hour of the morning, but you never knew. She was convinced that some kept up a twenty-four hour vigil. She opened the door carefully and stepped out into the misty grey garden. Beads of dew glimmered along the hedge and on the heads of the roses. It was quiet, except for the one lone bird, and very still. She took a deep breath filling her lungs with the morning air; she smelt damp grass and the heady scent of roses. She did quite like roses herself, not that she would ever say so to her mother, not now, though she might have before. Before Herbert. He had sliced her life in two, into before and after. Since they had come here she and her mother had been growing further and further apart. But this was no time to start feeling miserable; she must act.

The back door had to be left unlocked but it seemed unlikely burglars would arrive before Herbert got up, She tiptoed round the side of the house to the front, up the path, and out through the gate on to the pavement. The street was sleeping fast, all curtains drawn. A grey cat skulked along the opposite pavement. Ellen walked quickly now wanting to leave this bungalow land behind as soon as she could. She passed no one on the way to the main road.

She enjoyed the walk into the middle of the city. It felt marvellous to be out when everyone else was sleeping. How silly they were to be wasting these fresh, quiet hours! When she reached the Mound and saw Princes Street lying below she began to run. Freedom was in sight.

The last part of her journey was all downhill and she took it at a jog trot. Fife was still wrapped in morning mist but a few people were beginning to surface. A milk van passed, a car, a policeman on the beat. The latter gave her a quick look but appeared not to be interested.

Nicolas's street was undisturbed by any form of activity. Here she slowed her steps, went more warily, kept her eyes alert. She crept up the stairs, pased Mavis's flat holding her breath, and reached Nicolas's door without meeting anyone. In a second she was inside, closing the door, and then leaned back against it with relief and exhaustion.

Now that she was inside she must be extra quiet for there was Mavis to consider below. It meant she would be unable to play the piano but that she would have to accept as part of the price of not being at Herbert's. She tiptoed into Nicolas's spare room where she thought Mavis would be disinclined to go – there was no reason for her to – and pushed a chair against the door. Tomorrow, Monday, when Mavis was away at work, she would be able to emerge and wander around the rest of the flat, perhaps would even be able to risk playing the piano for a while. She unpacked the photographs of her father and Nick and placed them on the table beside the bed, then she lay down and within minutes was asleep.

EIGHT

Herbert did not waken till nine that Sunday morning. It was unusual for him to sleep so late but he had been restless during the night (he had eaten a tomato sandwich for supper) and at one point had wakened thinking the house was being burgled only to realise that he must have been dreaming. He pulled on his dressing-gown and went through to the kitchen to put on the kettle. He always made Rose a cup of tea on weekend mornings.

The morning was bright and sunny and two of his yellow roses were beginning to unfold. He wanted to go out and look at them close up. Should he nip out in his dressing-gown? Would the neighbours see? Well, what if they did? The thought came, surprising him. He tied his dressing-gown cord more firmly around his middle and made to unlock the back door. It was not locked. He frowned. He was sure he could remember locking it last night; he had never once forgotten, not even on the night his mother died. The lock was unlocked and the snib also drawn back. He opened the door and peered out gingerly as if he half expected a burglar might be lurking round the corner. The people two doors down had had their bungalow turned inside out three months back; it had made everyone on the street very cautious since. There was no one in the garden. He remembered again the faint noises in the night. Quickly he closed, locked and snibbed the door.

'Rose,' he called, going back to the bedroom, 'don't panic but I think we've been burgled.'

Rose shot out of bed at once, reaching for her house-coat. 'What have they taken?'

'I don't know yet. I've just found the back door open. They must have come in through a window.'

They went to the sitting room. It was dim and shrouded, the curtains were drawn just as they had left them last night. On pulling them back they saw that the windows were tightly shut, their snibs undisturbed. There were only two other windows a burglar could have come in by: the bathroom, if he was thin, and Ellen's, if he was not. The bathroom window proved untouched.

Herbert followed his wife to Ellen's room almost falling over her heels. She stopped in the doorway, her hand to her mouth.

'What is it, love?'

'Ellen's gone.' Her reaction was overdramatic, she realised that at once, and changed it to, 'She's not in her bed.'

Herbert gave a sigh of relief. That explained the opened back door. Ellen must have gone for an early morning walk. Rose nodded but did not look too convinced. Somehow it was not like Ellen although she would be the first to admit that one never could know what Ellen might get up to.

'Let's go and have our tea,' said Herbert.

On their way to the kitchen they saw the envelope standing on the ledge below the picture of Herbert's mother. The letter was addressed to 'Mrs H. Hall'.

'Mrs Hall,' she read. 'How strange! It looks like Ellen's handwriting.'

The writing was indeed Ellen's. Her mother had to sit down on a stool in the kitchen to read it and Herbert had to put three spoonfuls of sugar in her tea to help counteract the shock.

'She's run away! Oh, Herbert, what are we going to do?'

'What does she say?'

Mrs Hall read the letter aloud. 'I have thought about things for a long time and come to the conclusion that you would be better off without me. I know that you are supposed to be responsible for me until I am sixteen years of age so the best thing is for me to do this and relieve you of the responsibility as I know you would never do it yourself.' She paused to take a sip of tea. 'By the time you read this I shall be far away over the border. You are not to worry about me for as you are aware I am quite capable of looking after myself when I have to. The best of luck to you and Herbert in your new life. Love Ellen.' Mrs Hall flung the letter on to the table. 'Idiot!'

'But, love—'

'She'll be back. I know Ellen. She loves a bit of melodrama.'

'But where will she have gone?'

'Isadora's more than likely. Or Davie's.'

Mrs Hall cooked bacon and egg but Herbert's appetite was poor. He mangled the bacon and did not touch his egg.

'I'm sorry, Rose. I can't help thinking about Ellen.'

Rose went to ring Isadora's mother.

'No, we haven't set eyes on Ellen this morning,' said Mrs MacBain. 'Anything the matter?'

'No, nothing at all. She just went out for an early morning walk.'

'Ellen did? How strange!' Isadora's mother lowered her voice. 'You won't mind me saying so, Rose, but Ellen's been acting a bit strangely recently. Well, I know she always does a bit, but still. I was just saying to Isadora—'

Rose had to go, she'd left something on the cooker, could smell burning. She then rang Davie's mother.

Mrs Dunlop hadn't seen Ellen either, nor had Davie whom she called out to over her shoulder. She hoped Ellen wasn't in any kind of trouble? Trouble? Ellen's mother laughed. What kind of trouble could Ellen possibly be in?

'She's taken your marriage hard, you know, Rose. It's not easy at her age having a new man brought into her life, if you don't mind me saying so, especially since she was so fond of her father. He's always been her hero, hasn't he?'

Rose had to go, she'd left something on the cooker, could smell burning. She went to the kitchen to find Herbert staring mournfully out at the garden. He did not see his roses: Ellen's face came between him and them.

'I feel I've failed somehow, Rose. And I so much wanted to make a go of it. I'm so clumsy.'

'Oh, Herbert!' His wife put her arms round him. 'She's never given you a chance. She's such a stubborn girl.' She sighed. 'I think I'll have to talk to her about her father soon and put the record straight.' Herbert felt a bit alarmed at that proposal, it might upset Ellen even more. His wife said she would have to risk it and blamed herself for not having been brave enough to face the issue years before. Before things had got out of hand.

They went to church. Mrs Hall said that she was not unduly worried about Ellen – oh, she was a little of course – but by the time they got home they would probably find Ellen had returned and it was better to have something definite to do meantime.

Ellen had not returned when they came home. Her mother went again to phone to Isadora's and to Davie's. This time they answered so she was able to speak to them and not to their mothers. Isadora said that Ellen hadn't mentioned what she planned to do on Sunday and Davie said that Ellen had been very quiet the day before.

'Is anything wrong?' He sounded anxious.

No, no, Mrs Hall reassured him.

Herbert got the car out of the garage and they drove across town touring all the streets in the Fergusons' old neighbourhood, ending up in their own particular one. Isadora and Davie were leaning against the corner when they turned in and came up at once to the car to stand one on either side of it.

'Is Ellie lost?' asked Isadora.

'We haven't seen her since last night,' said Herbert gloomily.

'She's run away,' said Isadora. She straightened her back and spoke to Davie over the bonnet of the car. 'I told you so, didn't I?'

Mrs Hall got out of the car and began to cross-question Isadora wanting to know everything that Ellen had ever said on the subject of running away. Isadora told her that Ellen had thought of going to London.

'London!' said Herbert. 'That makes sense. She said in the letter she was going over the border.'

'She wouldn't have any money,' said Davie, kicking a stone in the road, his head bent down to watch it.

'She could hitch,' said Isadora.

'Hitch? Surely she wouldn't!'

'Now, Rose, don't take on so,' said Herbert. 'She is quite sensible if she wants to be, she said so herself.'

'I don't think she's feeling too sensible at the moment,' said Isadora.

At that moment Isadora's mother appeared on the pavement to find out what was going on and led Ellen's mother away for a drink of some soothing herbal tea. Herbert trailed after the two women, giving a miserable backward look at Davie and Isadora.

'I don't believe she'd go to London,' said Davie.

'That's because you've no imagination, Davie Dunlop, like I always tell you!'

Davie said he'd be seeing her and went off at a trot. He was going to have a go at finding Ellen; he had a hunch that she was still in Edinburgh, and that meant somewhere in this area. He knew all her haunts. He went along to the bridge at Stockbridge then took the path by the Water of Leith to St Bernard's Well. He remembered her saying once that she would like to live there: it would be her temple. She was not there. Only the man in charge was and he said he had not seen any girl answering to Ellen's description all day and, as Davie knew, she was rather hard to miss. For a while he sat on the bank waiting hopefully but she did not come. He moved on, continuing to take the path by the water to the Dean village. For a while he roamed about the old village going up and down its steep roads, investigating the mews, which, again, Ellen liked. They had often idled about here and she had said she wouldn't mind living in one of the little flats above a garage. These mews streets had a tucked away feeling, almost like being in the country. One or two men were lying on the ground working on their cars; several children were playing; two women sat gossiping beside a tub of geraniums. He asked them all. Had they seen a tall girl, almost six feet high, with red hair? They shook their heads, certain that they had not.

Back beside the water he went, to pause once more at the temple of Hygeia. The man shook his head decisively.

In Stockbridge he rested on the bridge scanning the river upstream, then crossed the road and looked downstream. A few kids from their year at school passed and he asked them too but they were sure they hadn't seen Ellie Ferguson either. He went now in the opposite direction taking the river path as far as Canonmills, after which he made for the Botanic Garden. It was busy: people thronged the paths and lay on the grass with their faces turned up to the sun. He scoured the gardens thoroughly going up and down every path, through the rock garden, round by the pond, along the rhododendron walks which were ablaze with startling pinks and reds; he went in and out of all the plant houses passing quickly from moderate temperatures to the moist sticky heat of the tropics where they had often lingered on cold winter days succumbing to accidie and revelling in the decadent look of the orchids, imagining themselves to be in the jungles of Malaysia or Brazil. He ended up in the Gallery of Modern Art. He zoomed over the polished floors taking no notice of the pictures today. No joy there. Nor in the sculpture garden either. He stood beside a large reclining figure of Henry Moore that Ellen especially liked (she said it made her feel petite) and surveyed the city skyline. It was most dramatic seen from this point, with the crouching lion shape of Arthur's Seat on the left-hand side, the rocky jagged castle on the right, and in between, towers and spires and cranes standing against the sky. He picked out the crown of St Giles and the slim Tollbooth spire. He had a feeling that if he waited at some favourite spot of Ellen's she would come. He willed her to come. His eyes were beginning to feel strained with staring. He blinked them rapidly several times and looked again. She had not come.

It would be so easy to miss her of course; it was an almost impossible task to make certain that she was not about somewhere. She might even hide behind a hedge or inside a clump of bushes if she saw him coming and did not want to be found.

He moved over to the edge of the sculpture garden where Epstein's figure of the Risen Christ stood sentinel. A finger of his left hand pointed to the open gaping wound in the palm of his right. Ellen always shuddered when she saw the wound, said she could feel the nails piercing her own flesh.

Oh, where on earth was she?

He descended to the sloping green lawn below and lay down now himself. The grass felt dry and warm. He closed his eyes.

After Davie left her, Isadora went to the café where she had arranged to meet Tom. He asked if she'd fancy going to Portobello for the afternoon: the fair would be open and he had some money in his jeans. But Isadora had other plans for their afternoon: they hiked up and down every single street in the area, along by the Water of Leith, up to Princes Street and through the gardens, down to Waverley Station, and then to the bus station at St Andrews Square. It was here, on the London bus stance, that Tom exploded.

'This is nuts!' he declared, folding his arms across

his chest and glowering at Isadora. She had made them waste a perfectly good afternoon, and all for what? Some wild goose chase after Ellie Ferguson! He couldn't care less if she'd taken off for Timbuctoo or had been sold for the white slave trade. Serve her right! In that case, she was finished with him, Isadora informed him in her iciest of manners.

Davie was wakened by a poke in the stomach from a deep dream in which he had been sitting in a Greek temple with a garland round his head drinking murky water from a well. He opened his eyes to see flashes of red and yellow at first and then he made out the pink and white face of Isadora against the bright blue of the sky. She was bending over him, the ends of her gold hair tickling his face.

'Wake up, Dozey!' She squatted beside him and he sat up rubbing his eyes and yawning. The cheek which had rested on the ground felt hot and marked by the grass. He felt slightly stunned. He looked at his watch and guessed that he must have slept for a couple of hours.

They exchanged details of their respective searches for Ellen and agreed that there was nowhere else they could go, nothing else they could do.

'I suppose she will come back,' said Isadora.

Ellen was so unpredictable and there were areas of her life they had never quite been able to understand. Like her father, for example, and talking to him as if he wasn't dead at all. He was alive to her, she had said sharply one day to Isadora; he kept her company and listened to her playing his piano. Isadora's mother who had been going through a spiritualist phase at the time had said how did they know he didn't?

'She wouldn't have gone to visit her father's grave or anything like that?' suggested Davie.

Neither of them knew where her father's grave was. Or how he had died.

'Maybe there were suspicious circumstances,' said Isadora.

But Davie, as she expected, scoffed at that idea. Irritated by the frustrations of the day and her quarrel with Tom for which she had not been prepared, she turned on Davie. 'Why do you never allow for anything out of the ordinary?'

Davie looked chastened, so she said quickly that she hadn't meant to tear a strip off him. 'No, you're right, Issie. Maybe I don't have enough imagination.' His large brown eyes, which usually were alive and merry, gazed at her mournfully like a sad cocker spaniel's. He had tried to use his imagination all afternoon, to visualise Ellen, follow her mind, and thus find out where she had hidden herself. For that must be what she had done. He didn't believe she had gone to London. And neither did Isadora, not really, when she began to imagine Ellen actually setting off. It was an act that belonged to Dick Whittington and his cat even though they knew that every year lots of girls ran away from home to go south. Isadora's mother had told them cautionary tales about such doings, as she did most things. She had heard stories about every conceivable catastrophe and always happened to bump into somebody's mother just after their son or daughter had suffered their particular catastrophe *and* regretted it.

'There is one other possibility,' said Isadora. 'Nick.'

Nick. That thought had come to Davie before he fell asleep on the warm grass but it had led nowhere for he had nothing with which to back up the name. That was all it was for him: a name.

'He's tall, dark and handsome, and quite old looking. Eighteen, Ellen said he was. Do you know any boys that would answer to that description? Think, Davie, think!'

Davie raked his memory, letting it range over school, playground, streets, cafés, parks, football pitches. Not a thing would come. He did not believe

110

he had ever come across anyone of the name of Nick apart from a kid in the next street with red hair who must be all of ten years.

'Hardly think he fits the bill!' Isadora sighed. 'Come on, let's go home. It must be tea-time.'

A rumbling sound came from the direction of Davie's stomach – he had just been about to go in for his lunch when Ellen's mother had arrived in the street with Herbert – and Isadora laughed.

Ellen's mother paced the small strip of carpet between the door and the window, up and down, up and down, until Herbert, a man not given to screaming, felt that he was on the brink of doing so for the first time in his life. He begged her to come and sit down, saying the usual thing about watching not bringing anyone any faster.

'But it's gone ten, Herbert!'

He said that sometimes Ellen came in even later, a foolish thing to say, for of course that had nothing to do with it. Ellen had been gone all day, since the middle of the previous night, as far as they knew. His wife said so and he apologised, which led her on to apologising for having snapped at him. Her nerves were fraying to the point of breaking. It had been a long day and had seemed even longer because it was Sunday and the street had been quiet and the postman had not called or the fishman. Distractions had been few and when the telephone had rung it had been either Isadora or her mother or Davie to ask the same question. Had Ellen come back yet?

'Would you like a cup of cocoa, Rose?'

Rose would not like a cup of cocoa. Herbert did not know what to offer next. Everything he could think of seemed to be wrong and when he had suggested phoning the police he had distressed her immensely. That had been two hours ago.

'We might just have to phone the police, dear.'

'Not yet, Herbert. If she's not back by midnight, maybe. But what could they do?'

Nothing much, he supposed, but it seemed better than doing nothing except pace the carpet and watch the road. He could hardly stand the sight of that strip of grey road running between the bungalows any more. 'Let me draw the curtains, Rose,' he said firmly. He went and did it, tugging them together tightly in the centre. If Ellen arrived she would let herself in. And now Rose was to sit down and let him make her a nice cup of tea.

She sat down. She looked exhausted.

They were drinking their tea when they heard steps on the garden path. Rose leapt up spilling her tea down the front of her going-to-church dress which she had not bothered to change. 'Ellen!' she cried. The door bell rang. It was unlikely to be Ellen who had a key of her own. 'The police,' whispered her mother. 'Something's happened to her, Herbert, I know it has!'

'Stay where you are, dear! I shall see who it is.'

Herbert shut the sitting-room door behind him and went to the front door. On opening it he saw on the doorstep the boy who had talked to them earlier.'

'Oh hello! You're Davie, aren't you?'

Davie nodded. His hands stayed in his pockets and his face had a kind of guarded look. Herbert invited him in.

Having heard so much about Herbert's bungalow, Davie found it familiar as soon as he stepped inside. It was almost like one of those dreams where you felt it had all happened before. The little sitting room crammed with furniture, the half-moon rug, the china cabinet, the ornaments on every ledge, and the portrait of Herbert's mother. His eyes went to that at once and were held fast by the woman's eyes. Ellen was right: they almost seemed to hypnotise you. He scratched the back of his neck.

'Any news, Davie?' asked Mrs Hall eagerly, imploringly.

He wished he could wave a wand and produce Ellen in the middle of the room, on the half-moon rug. He shook his head. Mrs Hall's brief burst of hope collapsed.

They sat him down on the settee between them, and offered him orange juice and coffee and biscuits, but he was not hungry. It was good of him to come, sighed Mrs Hall, she appreciated his concern and knew how fond he was of Ellen. Davie shuffled his feet a bit and looked as if he was on the point of saying something but didn't. Herbert eyed him.

'You don't know anything else that could help us, lad, do you?'

'Well—'

'If you do you'd better tell us.'

Both pairs of eyes were fixed upon him. He felt himself grow hot under his polo neck. Ellen would kill him but he would prefer that to her not being found again. And you never knew who or what that character was she was mixed up with.

'Isadora and I were wondering if she might be with her boyfriend.' He felt misery descend on him as soon as the words were out.

'Her boyfriend?' repeated her mother.

'Does she have a boyfriend?' asked Herbert.

Then he had to tell them everything else he knew which was not much. Mrs Hall seemed flabbergasted; she sat with her mouth sagging downward at the corners saying nothing. It was Herbert who cross-examined him.

'She goes to meet him every evening? Are you sure?'

'She says she does.' Davie half rose from the settee saying that it was time he went home, his mother would be wondering where he was. Herbert told him to sit back, he would run him home, he knew the bus service was not good on a Sunday and it was late even for a boy of Davie's age to be wandering around the city. Davie sat back. The only part of the bungalow that did not fully fit Ellen's description was Herbert himself. She had said he was dithery and unsure of himself and here he was taking charge, giving a feeling of being in command of the situation, in so far as he could be, given the circumstances.

'So you say he is tall and dark and goes by the name of Nick? We must presume also that he lives on your side of town since Ellen goes to visit him regularly.'

Perhaps Herbert had missed his vocation. Instead of Insurance he might have done well in the CID. His wife stared at him wonderingly.

'Nick.' Herbert spoke the name clearly, letting it fall amongst them. He repeated it. 'Ring a bell at all, Rose?'

She frowned, shook her head. Not that she could think of. Oh well, at least it was something, a small lead. Herbert stood up, brushing down the knees of his Sunday trousers which he too had not got around to changing. He would run Davie home now and Rose was to relax until he got back, then they would discuss their next move.

Mrs Hall listened to the car driving away. She sat back in the settee, letting her head fall against the thick brown velour cushion. It smelled musty. Perhaps new cushions would be an idea. She closed her eyes. Nick. Nicky. Nicolas. Nicolas!

She sat up. Surely the name of the old man whom Ellen helped was Nicolas? She went at once to the phone and dialled Mavis's number. Yes, said Mavis, he was called Nicolas but he was not at home, he was still convalescing.

'Oh dear!' Mrs Hall's hopes collapsed again. She went on to tell Mavis about Ellen's disappearance.

Hang on, said Mavis; she, like Ellen, had a key. She would go upstairs and look. Mrs Hall stood clutching the receiver staring at the picture of Herbert's mother on the wall. The eyes *were* extraordinarily penetrating. She made a face at them and then put her back squarely to the picture. Mavis was taking ages.

114

NINE

Ellen slept all morning after arriving at Nicolas's flat. On wakening she jerked upright in alarm forgetting where she was, not recognising the pale green room with the long dark green velvet curtains. An etching of an unknown city hung above the bed. Then she remembered that it was Nicolas's spare room. The city must be Prague. She lay back on the bed again.

It was nice in this room. The space was pleasing and the quietness soothed her. Turning her head she saw Nick's photograph on the table beside her. This would be where he would sleep when he came to Edinburgh. He would wake in the mornings and look at the pale green walls, the white cornices, the etching of the city. He would smile, stretch, and think of her. Yes, he would think of her and the hours they had spent together the day before.

She ate some biscuits and a piece of chocolate and then took up the two books she had put in her rucksack. She had bought them in a second-hand bookshop in Dundas Street the day before, had chosen them for one reason: they were about Paris.

The first one was called *Good Morning, Midnight* and was by Jean Rhys. There was a picture of a woman on the front in a cloche hat which almost covered one eye and a beaver lamb coat and she was drinking a glass of wine with her gloves on. She looked pensive and not at all gay as one might have expected her to look in Paris. She looked as if she had had a past. Ellen soon found that she had. A friend had rescued her from drinking herself to death in a

115

bed-sitter in Bloomsbury and now she had come to Paris to recuperate. Her life seemed to be full of darkness and terrible men. It was not quite the picture of Paris that Ellen wished to pursue. She put the book aside. Perhaps when she was older and had a past herself she might come back to it.

The other book was *The Narrow Street* by Elliot Paul, an American journalist who had gone to Paris in the twenties. There was a map in the frontispiece showing the Île de la Cité and the Seine; Nôtre Dame was marked, the Quai St Michel, the Rue de la Huchette and the Rue du Chat qui Pêche opening off it. The street of the fishing cat. That was the narrow street. Dawn was breaking behind Nôtre Dame, the cafés were opening up around the Place St Michel, the smell of coffee and French cigarettes was rising into the air, all sorts of interesting and unterrible characters were emerging from their alleys and garrets. This was more like it! Ellen became engrossed.

She read until her neck ached. She stretched, yawned. Her watch said half-past six; her stomach suggested midnight. She finished the biscuits and the chocolate. There were tins in Nicolas's store cupboard in the kitchen and a packet of opened Rice Crispies on the draining board. She was sure that Nicolas would not mind if she helped herself. Putting her ear against the floor she listened. She had not heard a sound from Mavis below all day. Sometimes she went to North Berwick on a Sunday with Olive who had a small car. They sat in the car and watched the people on the beach. The sun might well have tempted them today. Ellen decided to risk an expedition to the kitchen.

She went on tiptoe, pausing with held breath every time her foot found a squeaky board. In these old houses there was no lack of squeaky boards. Some of the people who had come to view their old flat had jumped up and down in the rooms to test the floors.

They had looked rather funny, as if they were bouncing on dead trampolines.

She had a snack of cold beans and peach halves in syrup, washed down with a drink of water, though afterwards she thought that she shouldn't really have run water for that was a sound that would travel. But she seemed to have got away with it on this occasion. After ten minutes she assumed that Mavis was either not in or had not heard for she did not appear. Ellen went back to the pale green room and the Left Bank of Paris.

Now she did not read but imagined herself and Nick walking up the Rue de la Cité together, hand-in-hand, pausing to admire the sun setting behind the spires of Nôtre Dame, continuing over the Petit Pont to turn into the Rue de la Huchette. They stopped to say hello to Henri, the proprietor at the Hotel du Caveau, and his wife Marie and Berthe his sister-in-law and Therese the cook and Georges the *garçon*. And look, Nick, here comes Madame Absalom who sells yarn and thread! What a fantastic name! Didn't he think it was a fantastic name? Everything was fantastic: the street, the smells, the people. And Nick. She looked *up* at him and he looked *down* at her and smiled.

A door slamming below broke her trance. Mavis had come home from North Berwick. Was there a murmur of voices? Ellen put her ear to the floor again and fancied that there was. Mavis might have brought Olive home for supper.

With the knowledge that Mavis was definitely underneath her Ellen found it difficult to think of herself with Nick any more. Mavis's face kept intruding. And her mother's. She itched to go and play the piano. It was only when she was playing that she could blot the world out completely.

The evening dragged by minute by minute. She tried again both the Paris of Jean Rhys and Elliot Paul and could not get involved in either. She was restless, wanted to walk, to run, to jump, to turn a somersault. She lay on the bed and stared at the shadowy ceiling. Having slept half the day she was convinced that she would not be able to sleep at all that night.

The light dwindled in the room, the street lights came on, cars passed sending stabs of light momentarily across the wall beside the window. After a bit she must have dozed.

'Ellen! Are you there, Ellen?'

She froze, legs spreadeagled, arms stiffening by her side. Mavis was calling her somewhere. And she was not dreaming. The room was almost black now, lit only by the street lamp outside.

'Ellen!' The cry came again, nearer.

The door of the room opened and a shaft of bright yellow light cleaved the darkness.

'Is that you, Ellen?' Mavis stepped back, uncertain that the figure on the bed was Ellen. Burglars did funny things sometimes, stopping for snacks and drinking bottles of wine before they departed with their loot. This time they might have decided to take a nap.

'It's me.' How could she deny it? She slid off the bed and stood before Mavis knowing all that Mavis was about to say.

'I've nearly been out of my mind all day,' said her mother, echoing Mavis's words when she arrived half an hour later.

'I'm sorry,' said Ellen dully. She felt terribly dull.

'You're sorry? Is that all you can say?'

What else? She only wanted to sleep. Herbert cautioned his wife to take it easy then he withdrew to the kitchen. Ellen had moved to the sitting room and had spent the time waiting for her mother by playing the piano.

'What did you think you were going to do, love? You don't really have a boyfriend, do you?' Ellen shook her head. 'You couldn't have stayed here.'

118

Nicolas would not have minded, said Ellen. Her mother told her not to be ridiculous, she couldn't live here with an old man on her own.

'He's younger than Herbert. Yes, he is! Inside.'

'You don't know Herbert. He's good and kind.'

'I never said he wasn't.'

'He's been worried sick about you.'

Ellen shrugged, her mother lost her temper. Understandably, said Herbert later, when they talked it all over. She got up and went to the piano where Ellen had placed the photographs of her father after coming through from the spare room. She regarded the smiling faces of her ex-husband.

'You simply can't go on like this, Ellen!' Impatiently she slapped them all face downward, one, two, three.

In a flash Ellen was up and across the room to rescue the pictures, clutching them to her with both hands. She was trembling. She turned them over.

'You've cracked the glass!'

Across the glass covering the big portrait head of her father was a zigzag splinter contorting his smile.

'I wish I could crack his head and all!'

'How dare you say that?'

'Because I was married to him, that's why.'

'I hate you! You're—' Ellen spluttered, backed against the wall, the pictures held tightly to her.

Mrs Hall sighed, moved towards her daughter, hand outstretched. She was sorry! But she had been very upset. Surely Ellen must realise what a terrible thing she had done to her?

'Come and sit down again, love, and let's talk.'

Reluctantly Ellen followed. They sat on two high armchairs a few feet apart. From the kitchen came the sound of Herbert clearing his throat. For a moment Mrs Hall did not speak; she seemed to be marshalling her resources.

'You know you'll have to come home with me, don't you, Ellen?' she said gently at last. 'I *want* you to come. I want you to give it a try, to give Herbert a chance. That's all I'm asking.'

'Have a good day at school?' asked Herbert.

'It was all right.'

'Any homework, dear?' asked Mrs Hall, peering at her knitting pattern and frowning. She was knitting Herbert a cardigan.

'History.'

'Herbert's interested in history, aren't you, dear? He might be able to help you.'

'I've done it.'

'What are you doing in history, Ellen?' asked Herbert.

'The Russian revolution.'

'Must say I enjoyed the Russian revolution.'

'Were you in it?'

'Now, Ellen!' Her mother gave her a little, reproving laugh.

'Nicolas had to leave Czechoslovakia because of the revolution. Well, sort of anyway.'

'Oh yes, Nicolas.' Mrs Hall looked up from the pattern. 'When's he coming home?'

'Tomorrow.' Ellen brightened.

'He won't need you any more now, will he?'

'Oh, but he does! We've got a bargain going. I help him with his chores and he teaches me the piano.' It was out before she could call it back. She could have bitten her tongue in annoyance at herself.

Her mother dropped a stitch. 'He teaches you the piano? I didn't know that, Ellen. You didn't tell me.' She continued for a few minutes, expounding on the need for honesty and trust between people, warming to her theme and allowing stitches to slide from her needle without even noticing. She was not the most expert of knitters, having knitted but one garment in her life before, to Ellen's knowledge, a jumper which had terminated around Ellen's ribs and come half-way down her arms.

Ellen stood up feeling suddenly constricted, having sat already too long in this tight family circle trying to make conversation. She really had tried, she felt. She stretched her arms wide and the fingers of her right hand caught the tail of a plaster duck. It swayed alarmingly, hovered for a moment in mid-flight and then crashed to the ground.

'Oh, I'm sorry!' The duck lay face down at her feet split into three pieces. Mrs Hall sprang up, losing the rest of the stitches on her needle.

'Honestly, Ellen, can't you ever—' She could go no further. She lifted the pieces of duck and fitted them together.

It didn't matter, said Herbert, it didn't matter at all. His wife said that of course it did, he had had those ducks a long time, they had belonged to his mother and Ellen would simply have to learn to be more careful.

'By the time I'm sixteen you'll have nothing left,' said Ellen, desperately attempting a joke and raising a wan smile from Herbert but none from her mother.

'I'll get you another duck, Herbert.'

'No, no, please don't bother, Rose.' He cleared his throat. 'Actually I have to confess . . . I never really liked them.'

Ellen looked at him with surprise. For a moment she almost liked him, but only for a moment. Something inside her would not let the liking last. 'That's all right then, isn't it? Doesn't matter, like you said.'

'Ellen!'

'But Herbert did say—'

'He was just trying to be nice.'

'He should say what he means then. I like people to be honest. Like my dad.'

'Your dad!'

'Yes, my dad. I know I'm not supposed to mention him—'

'*Mention* him?'

Herbert said why didn't he go and make them all a nice cup of tea? Ellen declared her intention of going to bed and her mother said that it would be as well if she did. She went, slamming the door behind her setting the two remaining ducks a-tremble on the wall. Herbert reached up and unhooked them. Three clean spaces showed on the wallpaper. He said that he truly never liked the ducks. He was beginning to find that there were a number of things he had never really liked. Amazing how you could go on for years accepting things that went against your grain and not even realise it. But Rose was in no mood at the moment to hear about his changes of heart: she was preoccupied with her daughter.

'But Ellen is impossible, Herbert! Like a four-year-old at times. Other times you'd think she was forty!' Mrs Hall sighed. 'I feel I'm a rotten mother.'

Herbert went to comfort her.

Nicolas sat in his chair by the window smiling happily. There was no sun to shine on him today, the fine spell had broken and the sky was overcast, but they had no need of sun in the room. They were both happy. Ellen had bought some French *pâtisseries* and made fresh ground coffee to celebrate his home-coming. And there had been a letter from Nick in the post. He was definitely coming. Dates and times were confirmed.

'You will like him, Ellen, I know it!'

He was coming in ten days' time. That meant he would still be here when the end of term dance was on.

'Nicolas, do you think—?' Nicolas looked at her inquiringly and she went on in a rush. 'Do you think Nick would like to go to my school dance with me?'

'He would be delighted. I will speak for him.'

Ellen found it all difficult to believe. It was like one of her daydreams that would cease when she stopped imagining. It did seem too good to be true. But there was Nicolas talking calmly and matter of factly about Nick and his visit wondering if the spare-room bed would need airing and the blankets washing. Ellen said she would take them to the launderette. And she would air the bed and clean the room.

'You can show him the sights of Edinburgh. The castle, Holyrood Palace, all the little closes off the Royal Mile, John Knox's house. He will want to see them all, I'm sure.'

Ellen smiled.

And now Nicolas wanted to hear what she had been doing on the piano in his absence.

Whilst Ellen was playing for Nicolas her mother was giving tea to Mavis who had a half-day off work. She poured from Herbert's mother's teapot which was admired by Mavis and passed her scones on a plate from Herbert's mother's wedding china.

'She had good stuff, didn't she?' said Mavis.

'Very.'

But Mrs Hall did not want to talk about her late mother-in-law. She said, 'I'm worried about Ellen, Mavis. If she starts going to Nicolas's again every evening the way she did before—'

'He's a very nice man, Rose,' put in Mavis quickly.

Rose did not wish to dispute that, she was sure he was delightful, but she did think it wasn't, well, it wasn't too healthy for a young girl to spend so much time in the company of an old man.

'She does spend time with her friends too, though, doesn't she?'

'But very little here with us.'

That was the crux of the problem, as Mavis realised, and she did see Rose's point of view. Ellen was seldom in for a meal, came home far too late across the town and paid little attention to any reprimand. What could her mother do? She couldn't go and drag her back forcibly.

'I think I shall have to stop her going to Nicolas's, Mavis.'

'Altogether?'

Rose was afraid so, they simply must have a chance, she and Herbert, to make a family life which included Ellen, and as long as she spent several hours a day after school at Nicolas's that would not be possible. Mavis sighed. Ellen was not going to like this but in the long run it might be for the best. Would Rose like her to speak to Nicolas? Mavis felt sure he did not realise the complexity of the situation, he was a good man and the last thing that he would want to do would be to contribute to their family problems. He had a strong sense of honour.

'Would you? That would be very good of you, Mavis. I'd been hoping you might, you know him so well. More tea?'

Mavis held out her cup.

Ellen lifted her hands from the piano keys and brought them back into her lap.

'Bravo!' Nicolas applauded. 'Very good indeed, Ellen.'

She spun around on the piano stool to face him. She knew herself that she had played well.

'Have I told you yet how pretty you are? I can see you now, Ellen, quite clearly. And I do like what I see.'

'What a lovely day it's been!'

It was time to let Nicolas go to bed, he was tired with the excitement of coming home. Just before she left he recollected something: he had found two books in his spare room, did not know how they could have got there. They were hers. She blushed a little, taking them, but decided not to tell him about her running away episode which seemed in retrospect rather infantile.

'See you tomorrow!'

She ran down the steps past Mavis's door which

124

looked firmly closed and out into the street. It was still quite light and too early to head for bungalow land; she would go and find Isadora and tell her that she was definitely going to bring Nick to the school dance. She found her with Davie in the café. Isadora was thrilled with Ellen's news, Davie less so. He sat with his elbows on the table and scowled at the stains on the formica.

'Who're you bringing now, Issie?' asked Ellen.

'Some Tom, Dick or Harry,' said Davie.

'Think you're funny, Davie Dunlop?' Isadora spoke now to Ellen. 'Malcolm.'

'Malcolm?'

'Canmore,' said Davie. 'King of the Scots. Hey, it's catching, Ellie!'

'Who're you taking to the dance, Davie?' asked Isadora.

'Me?' Davie didn't dance, and didn't want to either.

'Except with me on the top landing,' giggled Ellen. 'Swan Lake.'

He grinned.

He could still come to the dance, said Isadora, not being able to dance had nothing to do with it. There must be some wee girl he could bring. What about Agnes Ramsbottom?

'Or Ginny Malone? I'm sure she's sweet on you, Davie.'

'I'm glad I amuse you.'

'Oh, we're easily amused,' said Isadora. Her head turned as the door opened.

'There's Sweet William,' said Ellen.

'I shall definitely be going with Malcolm,' said Isadora in a loud voice.

'Come on and I'll chum you up to Princes Street for your bus, Ellie,' said Davie.

They said very little on the way. Ellen was thinking of all the improvements she must make to herself before Nick came: she must lose half a stone, get her hair thinned and perhaps dyed, swot up her French

125

verbs (especially the use of the subjunctive so that she could talk sophisticatedly to him), read some books by Balzac and Flaubert (so that they could talk intellectually). It was quite a lot to get through in a short time, she would have to begin at once and work systematically. As a beginning she could walk home and eat nothing when she arrived: that should get rid of a pound or two.

'I think I'll walk,' she said when they arrived in Princes Street.

'All the way? Don't be potty. It's miles.'

She was easily dissuaded, being tired and not fancying too much the long drag out through the suburbs. Davie waited beside her until the bus came. He too was thinking but about what she could not guess, unless it was Ginny Malone and the school dance, which was not probable. More likely to be about football. A sudden longing came over her.

'Hey, Davie, next time let's have a game in the street, eh? Of football.'

He nodded. She jumped on the bus looking back to wave and almost missed her footing. He grinned at her, shaking his head.

Her mother was up when she got in, trying to reconstruct Herbert's cardigan. Herbert had gone to bed having had a hard day at the insurance office.

'Want something to eat?'

Ellen shook her head. She was standing on the ramparts of the castle pointing out the landmarks of the city below to Nick. He wore a shirt with sleeves rolled up to the elbow and his arms resting on the parapet were a deep mahogany brown.

'Why don't you ask Isadora and Davie to tea one day? What about Wednesday?' Ellen started, she had been showing Nick how the Georgian New Town had been planned and laid out in geometric fashion with crescents and squares balancing each end of its major streets. Her mother repeated her question.

'They'd never find their way out here. Or back.'

Davie managed perfectly well, said her mother, that day when Ellen did her disappearing trick.

'Davie was out here?'

Her mother nodded.

'He didn't say. He's a deep one, Davie Dunlop. You never know what he's thinking,' said Ellen, speaking more to herself than her mother.

Her mother shrugged, rolled up the ball of fawn wool and stabbed it through with the knitting needles.

They went to bed without either the names of Herbert or Nicolas coming between them. They went to bed peacefully.

'Good night, dear.'

Ellen kissed her mother's cheek and went to dream of dark-eyed Nick.

TEN

Ellen came home early the following evening which pleased her mother. The only snag was that she and Herbert had planned to have an evening at the cinema. Ellen could come with them, she suggested, but Ellen had homework to do and was going to wash her hair.

'Funny,' said her mother as she and Herbert drove off. 'Not like Ellen to come home to do homework and wash her hair.'

It might be a turning point in a new Ellen, said Herbert.

'Mm,' said his wife.

The film was entertaining, they forgot Ellen for the space of three hours. They needed to forget Ellen sometimes, thought Herbert, as they sat eating mint humbugs in the darkness.

As soon as her mother and Herbert drove away, Ellen rushed to the plastic carrier that served as her schoolbag and took out the bag she had brought home from the chemist's. She read the labels on the two packets. Whilst the dye was taking she could do her moustache. She ran her forefinger lightly over her upper lip feeling the soft hairs ripple beneath it. She wanted to be flawless for Nick.

She painted the dye on with an old paintbrush, working according to instructions dividing the hair into sections. Just as well her mother had gone out! It would have been a problem to have locked herself in the bathroom for long enough without her mother tapping on the frosted glass to make sure she hadn't drowned. Her hair clung to her head looking like wet mud. The telephone rang.

'Oh hello, is that you, Ellen?' Mavis seemed surprised. 'You're not usually home so early.'

'I'm washing my hair,' said Ellen, watching the muddy coloured blobs dripping from her hair on to the pink hall carpet. It was a horrible shade of pink, a bit like the colour of bubble gum.

In that case Mavis would let her get on with it. She rang off deciding that she wouldn't go and speak to Nicolas yet. She had felt uneasy about the whole business all day and had wanted another word with Rose before she went ahead. But maybe now if Ellen was going to be reasonable and come home earlier. . . .

Ellen fetched a cloth from under the sink and scrubbed the dark spots on the pink carpet. Herbert's mother's carpet, naturally, and she had had it from the year dot until the day of her death. She watched Ellen scrubbing.

'Satisfied?' asked Ellen, looking up at her.

The answer was probably not.

It would have to do anyway; if she spent any more time on it then she would drip more dye at the same

128

time. She would have to hope that the remaining marks were just due to wetness and would dry before her mother and Herbert came back.

She returned to the bathroom. The wax had to be heated so she took Herbert's shaving mirror and the wax kit to the kitchen. She fancied this operation much less than the hair dyeing. Would it hurt? Only one way to find out, Davie would have said if he'd been here. She was glad that he was not. Turning the gas up high she heated the wax and before she could chicken out spread it across the offending area. She just about hit the ceiling. The wax was far too hot.

The telephone rang. She leapt like a kangaroo into the hall to answer it.

'Can you help with my physics?' asked Davie.

'No,' she bleated.

'What's the matter? Are you in pain?'

'Yes,' she said, and put down the receiver.

She went back to the kitchen to look in Herbert's shaving mirror. What a sight! And her lip felt stiff as a board. The telephone rang again.

'I say, Ellie, are you all right?' asked Davie.

'No! And don't phone again,' she mumbled as an afterthought before slamming down the receiver.

The moment had come – had passed, ideally – for the ripping off of the wax. She should have done it before it set too hard. It felt like a strip of concrete. She tugged the corner cautiously and yelped. She knew now why dogs yelped when they had their paws trodden on: if you couldn't speak, as she couldn't with the ridge of wax restraining her, then it was the only thing left to do. The telephone rang again but she let it ring, not caring, not interested. She leant against the draining board with perspiration streaming down the sides of her face, brown perspiration from the hair dye. What if she couldn't get the stupid wax stuff off? She might have to go to the Infirmary. She would *have* to get it off and the only thing for it was sheer brutality. The wax must be firmly taken hold of and yanked as hard as she could and never mind the pain.

After taking a deep breath she seized the corner of the wax moustache and pulled. She yelled. Her knees buckled under her like sandbags. But the stuff was off. She looked at it between the fingers of her right hand and saw, caught in it, some fine pale red hairs. They didn't look too many for all that agony. She looked back at herself in the mirror. Her upper lip was a fiery red, but hairless; and it ached like someone had just put a branding iron to it. She sluiced cold water over her mouth again and again seeking relief, getting it for a moment but then the fire started up again. She was beginning to feel quite ill.

A cup of coffee and a chocolate biscuit restored a little of her strength. Her lip still felt terrible but she told herself that it would die down in time. She held the back of a large tablespoon to it.

The telephone rang again.

Davie wanted to know if Herbert had been beating her up? Did he really think Herbert would be able to? asked Ellen, talking with the tablespoon still held in place. Well, maybe not, admitted Davie, but he had been dead worried about her. She had sounded as if she had been in dreadful pain.

'I was. I'd burnt myself.'

'Oh, I see. Can you help me with my physics now then?'

'Not now, Davie.' She noticed the drips were coming faster and faster from her hair and running all down the plastic apron she had tied about her shoulders. 'I'll ring you later.'

It must be time to wash off the dye. She hoped she wouldn't have to go through this procedure too often; if she did it would age her before her time and defeat the object of the exercise which was to make her look desirable. She giggled, steadied herself against the basin. The liquid coming off her hair did not seem at all chestnut-coloured, more like khaki, but she

130

presumed that was nothing to go by. She shampooed her head three times, rinsed it and then wrapped it in a towel. Her upper lip still ached furiously.

Above the bath was a first aid cupboard. Raking amongst the dozens of tubes and bottles (they charted Herbert's mother's illnesses throughout the years, everything from corns to earache) she found anti-burn cream. It was orange-coloured but she smeared some on and found it did seem to help a bit. Now she had an orange moustache. What women got up to in pursuit of beauty! Whenever she'd seen her mother looking like Frankenstein's granny in a white face pack she had thought she was an idiot. And just look at her!

'Ellen!' called her mother, coming into the hall. They had had a good evening at the cinema and she felt refreshed. She frowned down at the marks on the carpet. 'Where are you, Ellen?'

There was no answer and the sitting room was dark. She must have gone to bed, said Herbert, his eyes also on the marks.

Mrs Hall opened Ellen's door an inch and whispered, 'Ellen, are you awake?'

Mutterings from within encouraged her to switch on the light. Ellen was in bed but her head was not visible.

'You all right, dear?'

Ellen's head shot up in the bed like a jack-in-the-box. 'No,' she said. 'I'm not.'

Her mother let out a cry which brought Herbert hastening to her side. He stopped in the doorway and stared.

'Latest fashion,' said Ellen. 'How do you like it?'

Her hair was an odd shade of green and her upper lip bright orange.

'What have you done to your beautiful hair?' cried her mother.

'I've dyed it.'

131

'Dyed it? Oh, Ellen! And it was such a lovely rich shade of red.'

Ellen stared at her mother. 'You might have told me that before. I've always hated my hair.'

What a silly girl she was! Her mother flapped her hands and Herbert stole off to the kitchen to get the cloth from under the sink to wipe the marks from the carpet. He noticed the cloth was dirty and streaked with mud-coloured blotches so he tried to wash it out first. It would not come clean. Nor would the carpet which he rubbed vigorously with a piece of old sheet and, as he squatted on his haunches staring at the mess, he began to realise how the marks had come there in the first place.

'We'll get a new hall carpet,' he said to his wife in the morning. 'I've always fancied a change.'

Ellen did not got to school – how could she looking like that? – and as soon as the hairdresser's was open Mrs Hall rang and made an appointment for her to go and have her hair re-dyed, back to its original colour or as near as possible.

'It's amazing what they can do.'

'I hope so,' wailed Ellen. 'They'll need to be good on miracles.'

So she spent half the day at the hairdresser's reading magazines – but not the beauty hints. She was finished with those. Nick would have to take her as she was or not at all. She comforted herself by thinking that Nicolas thought her pretty and his nephew seemed to take after him in many respects. In looks, height, and love of music.

After Ellen had gone to the hairdresser's Rose rang Mavis at her work. She was secretary to an architect and at the moment business was slow. Mavis was often glad of a chat to help pass the time and Rose needed to get Ellen's latest doings off her chest, after which they both had a good laugh.

'Do you remember when you dyed your hair purple?' said Mavis.

Rose sobered and asked if Mavis had spoken yet to Nicolas. So Rose still wanted her to then? Mavis's voice sounded gloomy.

'Herbert and I have talked it over, and do you know what, Mavis? He's suggested paying for piano lessons for Ellen!'

'But not from Nicolas?'

'Well, hardly.'

The architect came into Mavis's office; she had to go. 'I'll attend to that for you immediately, madam,' she said and put down the receiver.

Ellen emerged from the hairdresser's looking more or less returned to normal. Even her lip had subsided. Since there was not much point in going to school now she went to Nicolas's. He laughed loud and long at the tale of her doings although, of course, she did not tell him for whose benefit she had waxed off her moustache (her mother had said she was silly, again, that she didn't have a moustache, everyone had a few hairs on their upper lip) and dyed her hair. She had an extra-long piano lesson and made lasagne and then he played for her whilst she reclined on his pinkish-red chaise-longue. When Nick came she would recline thus in the long green dress and Nicolas would play as he was doing now.

'See you tomorrow!' he said, when she got up to go.

But when she came on the tomorrow he looked solemn, even sad, with not a hint of the gaiety of the day before. Was there anything wrong? she asked quickly. Sit down, he said, he wanted to talk to her, he had been thinking. The words sounded ominous and the sadness in his eyes petrified her. She perched on the edge of a chair and stared at his face.

'I've been thinking, Ellen, that you spend too much time with me.'

'Is that all?' she cried. 'Don't be silly, Nicolas! I don't mind how much time I spend. Anyway, what do you spend on me?'

He leaned back in his chair and closed his eyes momentarily.

'Are you sure you're all right?' She came to crouch in front of him.

'Yes, I'm fine. Just tired.'

She began to scold him saying that he had probably been doing too much since he came home, he should take things easier.

'Perhaps you are right. Perhaps I need to take things easier.' He looked away from her, passing his hand across his forehead as if he had a headache.

'Do you want . . . . ? Would you prefer me to go, Nicolas?'

'Perhaps that might be best.' Still he did not look at her.

For a moment Ellen did not speak, then she asked, 'Is it too much for you . . . teaching me? You must tell me if it is.'

'Sometimes,' he said in a strangely helpless voice that she had never heard from him before. He was usually so calm and so sure. But she supposed nobody did feel calm all of the time. He was so clumsy, he said, she must forgive him, he did not know how to say this.

There was no need now: she had the message. She stood up. He felt he had had enough. Well, she could understand that. It was not quite like that, he protested, he had enjoyed teaching her but the operation had taken more from him than he had expected. After all, he was seventy years old. No spring chicken, eh?

'It's all right, really. I'll still come in and make your tea though, if you'll let me.'

'There's no need now, Ellen. I can cook a little myself and Mavis is very good.'

'Mavis! Perhaps you'll marry her.'

He smiled. 'I hardly think so.'

'Why not? Everyone else is getting married.'

'Ellen, listen! For a while I've been feeling I've been taking you away from your home too much.'

'My mother hasn't been here, has she?'

'No. I have never met your mother. But you see, Ellen, we couldn't go on as we were. We weren't being very realistic. Perhaps we were playing games a little, pretending time didn't exist, forgetting that you had a duty to your mother and your own home.'

Ellen looked at him levelly. 'Are you sure my mother hasn't been here?'

'Cross my heart!'

She smiled bleakly. That was it then, nothing left for her to do but go. He would still like her to visit him, perhaps once a week, and they could have a long lesson then. She shrugged, as if uninterested, saying she wouldn't want to trouble him.

'Ellen! I want you to come. And anyway, there will still be my young nephew coming in ten days' time.'

Yes, there would still be Nick. Her heart lifted. She might go back to Paris with him, run away from all these other exhausting considerations. She could get a room in the Rue du Chat qui Pêche and a job in one of the cafés on the Boul' Miche.

The doorbell rang.

'That'll be Mavis,' said Ellen.

'I'll go.'

She sat down on the piano stool, began to play, and to sing very softly.

> 'They call me the gooseberry
> 'Cos I'm always alone
> While the other two whisper
> And want to be on their own.'

But when Nick came she would no longer be a gooseberry. They would walk hand in hand and whisper on their own.

Nicolas came in with Mavis.

'Hello, love,' said Mavis.

'Hi!' Ellen lifted her plastic carrier bag. 'I'll be off then, Nicolas.' She went with quick goodbyes, without looking back.

Nicolas sat down, his body seemed slack. 'Well, I've done it, Mavis.' And was he upset? Mavis could see

135

that he was, felt contrite now, was uncertain that she should have asked him to do what she had. 'I loved her coming, she brought life into the room. But you were right, Mavis, I was not giving Herbert a chance and he must have one.' He closed his eyes.

'Are you all right, Nicolas?'

'Just tired. And old.'

Rose said goodbye to Mavis and put down the receiver. So it was done! She went to the back door to call to Herbert who was working in the garden. He appeared round the side carrying a large fork over which dangled something clogged with earth. His wife shuddered. What did he have there? Giant worms?

He came to the door, his eyes riveted to the end of the fork. A frown corrugated his forehead. 'Rose, they look like Mother's pearls.'

'Your mother's pearls?'

He reached out and unhooked the dangling muddy rope. Unquestionably they were pearls, and his mother's. They lay in the palm of his hand glinting feebly through their layer of dirt. He had dug them up round the side, near the hedge.

'How strange! Ellen must have dropped them.'

'They were pretty deep down. Looked as if they'd been buried.'

'Buried? I'm sure Ellen wouldn't. . . .' Her voice trailed off. She would take them and clean them. She began to apologise, for Ellen, but he cut her off saying he had a feeling Ellen hadn't taken to the pearls. Maybe they were too old for her and they should put them away until she was older and could appreciate them. His wife smiled at him. What a good idea! She took the pearls and rinsed them under the tap, then wrapped them in a serviette to put away in the bottom of a drawer.

Herbert pulled off his gardening boots and followed her inside. They had a cup of tea sitting at the kitchen table with the door open on to the garden letting in the scents of evening. Stock and phlox and delphiniums and roses. The garden might be small but it gave her enormous pleasure. Herbert didn't know how much it meant to her to be able to open a door and step out on to the ground without first having to descend three flights of dingy, grey, smelly stairs.

They talked about Ellen − they always seemed to be talking about Ellen − and she told him that the arrangement with Nicolas had now been severed. Herbert said they must arrange the piano lessons immediately to fill the gap, Rose should go tomorrow and have a word with the wee woman round the corner who taught Wendy and Debbie and was reputed to be very conscientious and painstaking. She hesitated. She wondered was it really wise to go ahead, wouldn't it be more advisable to let the piano go entirely? Ellen might do better to concentrate on the 'cello. Her teacher said she showed promise but did not practise enough.

'Come on now, Rose. That's just an excuse, isn't it? Not to let her play the piano? You'll need to get over all that yourself, won't you?'

Sighing, she admitted that she would. Yes, it was time. And before she did she knew she must tell Ellen the truth about her father, it lay on her conscience like a millstone. But if Ellen was to learn the piano, where would she practise? Herbert thought they might be able to throw something out and get the piano in here but his wife would not let him do that. Ellen could practise at the Dunlops, Davie's mother did not mind, and then they would see. One step at a time. At the moment she could not face the idea of her ex-husband's piano coming back into her life.

Ellen came home and totally rejected the offer of piano lessons from the wee woman round the corner. After having someone like Nicolas? Never! She went to bed.

'You see,' said Mrs Hall, 'how impossible she is.'

'Nicolas does seem to be pretty special,' said Herbert wearily.

Ellen seldom came home in time for their evening meal even though she no longer went to Nicholas's and when she did arrive she was silent and uncommunicative though very polite. After a few minutes she would retreat to her room where she closed the door and played records so quietly that not even a mouse could have protested. Her mother felt despairing.

'I shall speak to her on Saturday, Herbert. I can't wait any longer.'

On Saturday morning Ellen lay in bed reading about the people of the Rue du Chat qui Pêche and the Boul' Miche. The sun shone on the garden but she could not be bothered to get up. She would rise at lunchtime then cross the city to meet Davie and Isadora.

A tap on the door, and her mother appeared carrying a tray. She had brought Ellen breakfast in bed. Ellen protested saying she shouldn't have, it wasn't her birthday or anything. She glanced uneasily at her mother.

Mrs Hall sat down on the edge of the bed. Ellen drank the orange juice and began to eat the bacon and egg. She felt a bit like the condemned man and his last supper. Something unpleasant was coming up, she knew that from her mother's face, but felt indifferent for nothing worse could happen than had done already. In a way that was a comfort. The rest of life should be, if not easier, then less harrowing.

'There's something I should have told you a long time ago, dear.' Her mother looked up at the three smiling faces of Ellen's father.

'Is it about my father?' The knife fell with a clatter on the plate. Ellen pushed the tray aside.

'I've kept meaning to and kept putting it off.'

'Perhaps you don't need to then.'

'No, no, I must. Ellen, this is going to come as a big shock to you — but your father is not dead. He is still alive.'

ELEVEN

'He's alive?' cried Ellen.

An upsurge of joy such as she had never before known swept through her, banishing her lassitude and indifference to the day. It had suddenly become golden. She leapt out of bed. And then she became strangely calm for, after all, it was only what she had expected, what she had been waiting for all these years. She had always felt that her father was not dead; it was they who had scorned her, glanced away uneasily when she had talked of him as if he were alive. 'So I was right all the time?'

Her mother shifted uncomfortably. 'Well, I don't know if you could put it quite like that. It's more complicated. He's in Australia.'

Ellen smiled, flung open the window, drank in the smell coming from a rose bush beneath. Where he was was a mere detail. At least he was on this earth. As long as he was, all other complications could be overcome.

'That's where he went when he left us.'

'He *left* us?' She whirled round.

'Yes. He went off with another woman.'

'I don't believe it. He wouldn't do that. Go away and leave us!' Ellen laughed. She remembered him hoisting her up on to the top of the piano where she sat whilst he played and sang. He sang songs that he made up especially for her. He had made up stories for her too about exciting things the two of them could do together.

'But he did, Ellen. You were only three so you don't remember. No, you don't,' she said more vigorously, crushing Ellen's protests. 'You were so small I thought it best to tell you he was dead. You would understand that better. I meant to tell you the truth when you were older but you built him up into such a hero. You see, I hadn't bargained for that.'

'You should have told me! You had no right to lie to me. I could have written to him.' Then she would have been able to prove to everyone that she had a father.

'He didn't write to you, dear,' said her mother gently.

Ellen turned on her, demanding to know how she could be sure that was the truth. She might lie about everything that suited her convenience. Her mother shook her head. She was done with lying; only the truth was of any use now. There had never been any letters for either of them. He might not have wanted to upset her, suggested Ellen. That could be true, her mother acknowledged.

'But you do know he's still alive?'

Apparently Mavis saw his cousin sometimes, got news of him that way. It would be possible then to get his address? Mrs Hall supposed so. Ellen meant to write straight away, to let her father know that *she* was alive and remembered him and wanted to see him. He might send the money for her fare to Australia.

Her mother did not comment.

'He was fond of me, wasn't he?'

'Yes, but—'

'But what?'

'He always had to do what *he* wanted, Ellen. There's something else.' Ellen waited. Her mother went on, 'He's got four other children. By his second wife.'

Ellen sat down, putting her back to the open window. A fresh breeze grazed the nape of her neck making her shiver.'He's got four *other* children?'

Her mother nodded.

'Boys or girls?'

'Girls. All girls.'

The nightmare was closing in again, the dream had gone. Her father was not alive. He had four other daughters for whom he played and sang and smiled.

She got up and turned down his three smiling faces. She felt perfectly composed.

'I think I'll get dressed now.'

'Ellen—'

'Don't say anything else, *please*. I don't want to speak about him ever again. As far as I'm concerned, he *is* dead.'

Her mother and Herbert went off to do the Saturday shopping. Ellen got dressed and left the house. She walked into town. She needed the exercise, the steady movement, so that her mind could flow unchecked and come to terms with what her mother had told her. To begin with she had felt numbed and extraordinarily calm. So her father was in Australia with four other daughters! Well, what of it? And then the numbness thawed and she felt pain, pain at having been abandoned in favour of four others, after which followed anger, sharp and fierce, which made her walk with longer, faster strides keeping time with the silent drumming in her head: *I hate him; I hate him; I hate him.* Anger faded back into pain which caught her throat and brought a tightness across her chest. By the time she reached Princes Street she felt dulled again and did not know what to think or feel. She went to Nicolas's.

Nicolas listened intently and when she finished sat quiet for a while. She watched him. Eventually he said that he did not know whether to feel pleased or sorry for her.

'You should be pleased, shouldn't you? My father is alive and not dead.' Now she could feel the life that was in her father extending across the world to reach her. She wanted to go to him at this moment.

'But he's as good as dead, for you, Ellen. Well, is he not?'

'No! I'm going to go to Australia to find him. I must see him. And surely he will want to see me – his own daughter?'

'He has four others.'

141

'What difference does that make?' Her tone was defiant. Those four faceless unnamed girls were all younger, she had come first: that must mean something.

Nicolas thought that if her father had wanted to keep in touch he would have somehow. He might have written, countered Ellen, and *she* might have burnt the letters. Her mother had lied enough, hadn't she?

'She lied to protect you. Oh, wrongly, I believe, but I understand why she did it, and maybe your father did what he did for the best too. He might have thought it better to make a clean break, put the past behind him.'

'You think that's what I should do too, don't you? But I've got to find him again, Nicolas, I've got to!'

What if she found he was a stranger and not at all the man whom she remembered coming home from the pub smiling, playing tunes for her on the piano, telling funny stories? She would get to know him again, he was still her father, and that could not be changed. Admitted, conceded Nicolas. But what of his new wife and their children? She could not ignore them.

'They are his life now, Ellen. It's going to be hard for you to recognise that but you must! It's impossible to pretend otherwise.'

She was trembling. He watched her hands flutter by her sides then grasp one another behind her back; the fingers locked pulling as in a tug of war.

'Would you like me to give you a lesson?'

She shook her head. Today was not a day for playing the piano. She needed to be on the move again.

'Take care!' he said, unable to say any more.

After she had gone he went over to his piano and began to play. He played until Mrs Hall arrived.

'I hope you don't mind me coming? I'm so worried about Ellen. You see, she just went off without a word.'

He did not mind at all, he assured her, was pleased to meet her at last. He invited her into his sitting room and gave her a glass of madeira.

'It's a lovely room,' she said, looking round, relaxing a little. Her face was tight and anxious. 'I can see why Ellen liked to come so much.'

'Thank you.'

'Have you seen her?' He nodded. 'I thought she might have come here. She thinks a lot of you.'

'And I of her.'

'You've been a kind of – well, father-figure to her.'

Nicolas said that he had never wished to deprive her husband of that role and she came back quickly saying she realised that and had not come to reproach him, far from it. He thought he had been a bit selfish though, allowing her to come so often. She protested and he shrugged.

'We all see things from our own point of view, don't we?'

'Yes we do.' She smiled at him. She liked him and the liking had been immediate. How strange when the very sound of his name had previously invoked such strong feelings of resentment in her.

How was Ellen? she wanted to know. Confused: that was the only answer he could give, and on leaving him she had been consumed by the idea of seeing her father again. She had left him to go walking, he imagined, and her mother might well find her along by the Water of Leith. She made to rise but he asked if she would stop a moment, he wished to talk to her about something very important.

'It's about Ellen and her music.'

She sighed, bit the edge of her lip.

'I know it's a painful subject, it opens up old wounds – forgive me for speaking so frankly – but you must face it, mustn't you? For Ellen's sake.'

Ellen sat on the balcony with her back to the temple of Hygeia, feet flat on the ground, knees in the air. There were no boys fishing today and only an occasional walker passed giving her the briefest of glances. On the other side of the valley the trees grew high and thick shielding the streets that climbed the hill. She was back to feeling drained. She watched the water ripple, listened to its splash and gurgle and to the far-off sound of traffic and call of small children playing. She sighted a bird hovering on a branch overhanging the water. It swayed as though mesmerised. The water and the bird and the humming sounds mesmerised her. Her father was far far away, in Australia. Down under. Dead and buried.

After a while – quite a long time – she got up feeling stiff-kneed and slightly chilled. She walked back to Stockbridge and went towards the Botanic Garden. The luxurious tropical hothouses called to her promising heat and torpid languor and a removal from the sharp-edged stone city.

As she came along by the railings surrounding the gardens, the black iron railings that bewildered her eyes by the rapidity of their passing, she became aware of steady footsteps behind her, steps which were quickening, catching up on her. She glanced back. Her mother was following her, walking faster than was her custom, breathless with the unusual exertion. Ellen began to run.

She ran all the way to the gate, passing the navy-blue suited man in his box, and turned into the garden. She ran all the way to the glasshouses coming first to the oldest one, built in Victorian times, and to her the most beautiful. It housed the great giant palm trees. She went inside. Impossible to run now. She drifted under the high palm fronds resisting the temptation to linger and inhale the smell of damp earth and other, strange, indefinable smells. Beyond the glass she saw a blur that might be her mother. Swiftly she moved into the next house and across it into the next. The air was warmer and heavier here. This was where the orchids and cycads grew and luxuriated. Her limbs slowed. Outside a wind blew which she registered only now in contrast to the stillness inside. Water dripped. *Spathiphyllium commutatum*. White flowers. From Malaysia. *Encephalartos natalensis*. Giant fronds. From South Africa. She felt removed to different worlds.

'Ellen?' Her mother's voice, pitched low in order not to attract the wrong attention, brought her back to this one.

She ducked her head under a giant frond, stood still.

'Ellen? There you are!'

'Giant orchid. Stockbridge.'

'What a silly you are!' Her mother breathed deeply, to recoup lost breath and ease the feeling of suffocation that the steamy heaviness of the atmosphere gave her. 'Come on, let's get out of here. I can hardly breathe.'

It seemed cold outside. Ellen shivered but her mother was relieved. She would hate to go to the tropics. She led the way to an empty seat where they could talk in peace. Patting her chest, she said that she must be getting old.

'Mind you, you gave me a fair run for my money.'

'I'm sorry.'

'No, *I*'m sorry, love. I did something pretty terrible to you. I've been thinking about it — Herbert made me really — and do you know what I've come to realise? That I wanted your father dead?' She returned Ellen's look. 'Yes, I did. Because of what he'd done to me. So by saying that he was, it was the next best thing.'

Ellen nodded.

'But you kept him alive for me,' said her mother ruefully. 'You wouldn't let him lie down and die.'

'I'm sorry.'

'You don't have to say sorry, Ellen.'

'But I've been pretty silly. I hate him now!' she burst out, disturbing a flock of tiny birds that were waiting hopefully near their bench. They rose up into the air in a cloud and winged away to the nearest tree.

'I don't want you to hate your father, dear. It was all a long time ago, it's past. In time you'll feel it's past too.'

'I wouldn't go to Australia now even if he begged me to. Oh, I know he's not likely to. He wrote me off!'

'That's hard to accept, I know. But I've got over it at last. And I've got Herbert now. He's a far better husband to me than your father ever was. And he'd be a good father to you if you'd let him.'

Ellen watched the birds coming back. They were always ready for another try, seemed to be enormously optimistic. The birds in the garden were well fed. She and Davie had spent many hours with bags of bread for birds and nuts for squirrels, roaming over the entire part not wishing to favour one settlement of birds more than another although Davie often declared he recognised the birds and that they were following them.

Ellen said that she didn't think Herbert would be too keen on her now, she had been pretty nasty to him, after all.

'He's a tolerant man. He might be a bit set in his ways but he's more open-minded than you think.'

'It was probably his mother.'

His wife smiled. 'Mothers can be pretty awful at times, can't they?'

They laughed and her mother took Ellen's hand and squeezed it.

'Shall we go home now? Don't know about you but I'm hungry. And Herbert will be anxious, about us both.'

They found Herbert half in and half out of the sitting room struggling with his mother's china cabinet. His face was brick red.

'Herbert, what are you doing?'

'Moving the china cabinet.'

'But where to?'

'The garden shed.'

His wife opened her mouth to begin protesting but

146

Herbert was more interested in the cabinet and was giving orders to Ellen, telling her to take the end and help him swing the thing round the corner. These bungalows had such damned narrow doorways. 'Right, easy does it. Round a bit to the left, Ellen, there's a girl. Fine, fine.' Mrs Hall stood back out of the way, quite astonished. The cabinet made the bend round the door and stood in the hallway filling it. They pressed themselves against the wall. Ellen's head knocked the picture of Herbert's mother askew. He put up his hand and took it down. 'Now to get it out of the back door. Are you fit, Ellen? OK, heave-ho!'

They each took an end of the piece of furniture which had been emptied of its china and moving carefully edged their way from the hall into the kitchen, round the table and out of the back door, followed by Mrs Hall who was wondering if Herbert had been sitting in the sun without a hat on. Did he know what he was doing? she ventured to ask. Certainly, he said, pausing only briefly to answer.

The china cabinet was carried into the shed where it took up most of the floor space. Herbert moved the garden forks and rakes back against the end wall.

'It'll be damp in the shed.'

'Who cares about that?'

'The cabinet might warp.'

'I was thinking I might sell it.'

'Your mother's cabinet?'

'It's not mine though, is it?' said Herbert and led the way back inside the house.

The sitting room looked strangely empty with the cabinet gone. There was a blank space against the wall where it had stood since the day Herbert's mother came home from her honeymoon at Fort William. They gazed at the space.

'What are you going to put in its place, Herbert? It looks kind of bare.'

'Ellen's piano.'

'My piano?'

Herbert rubbed his hands and smiled, well pleased with his surprise. 'That's right. Your piano. You don't want to have to go playing in other people's houses. You should be able to play in your own home.'

Ellen did not know what to say; she was stunned, as, it appeared, was her mother.

'There should just be room to fit an upright in here, shouldn't there?' said Herbert.

'Oh yes,' said Ellen. 'The only thing is — I don't know if I want to bring my father's piano in here. In fact, I don't think I ever want to touch it again.'

Her mother thought she might change her mind in a day or two, once she had got used to things. Ellen could think it over, said Herbert, there was no hurry and if she decided she didn't want to bring in the piano then he would buy her a new one, well, maybe not brand new but he could afford a good secondhand. He'd been pricing one or two in a piano shop.

'You'd buy me a piano? Oh, Herbert!' Ellen flung her arms around his neck before she realised what she was doing. She laughed, feeling a little bit embarrassed, and Herbert laughed, feeling very pleased.

Well, what a day! Mrs Hall had to sit down. Herbert decided they needed a small sherry to celebrate or calm their nerves or whatever. Ellen too: she might have a small one, might she not? Her mother nodded.

'What's happened to your mother's picture, Herbert?' she asked. There was a blank space on the sideboard.

'It was getting a bit crowded there. Thought we might put it through in the hall.'

Herbert's wife smiled a very small smile and sipped her sherry.

'Do you know something, Rose?' Herbert spoke solemnly. 'I feel as if I've been liberated.'

'Liberated? Whatever do you mean?'

'Do you mean from your mother?' put in Ellen.

'Ellen!' Her mother reproved her quickly and automatically.

148

'No, she's right, Rose. By Jove, she's right! It's as if – well, as if I'd been locked in all these years—'

'Restricted?' said Ellen.

'Yes. And now I'm not!' He laughed. 'Freedom's heady stuff, isn't it?'

Ellen nodded.

Rose felt she needed another glass of sherry. Whilst she drank it she watched Herbert, who sat with a very bemused smile on his face, and from time to time laughed, out loud.

Ellen slipped off to her bedroom. She had something to do. She lifted up the three photographs of her father which she had put face downward earlier and looked at them. He remained unchanged, ageless, without a care. It was the last time she would ever look at them.

The door opened, her mother put her head in to say tea was almost ready. She stopped, seeing the photographs in Ellen's hands.

'It's bound to hurt for a while, love. Perhaps for quite a long time.'

'I don't ever want to see his stupid face again! I want to burn them.'

'Tell you what, why don't you put them away somewhere, in the bottom of a drawer, forget them, and then one day you might be able to look at them again? You might want to.'

Ellen shrugged. She did not care. Her mother lifted the photographs and took them away to lie beside the pearls of Herbert's mother. When she came back she found Ellen still standing by the window staring into the garden.

'He's gone his way, Ellen. We must go ours.'

Ellen nodded.

'He might come back to see you one day, Ellen,' said Nicolas. 'From what I've heard of him he seems unpredictable.'

'I wouldn't see him if he did.'

'I wouldn't count on that. Knowing you, I imagine your curiosity would get the better of you.'

That raised a grin and she came to sit near him. She felt better today, though sadder. It was the sense of loss that she was most aware of: she no longer had her father to talk to, he no longer watched over her.

'Odd, isn't it? All the years when he was thought to be dead he was alive for me and now it's the other way round.'

It would take time to get used to coming home and not greeting him, telling him what she'd done that day, playing for him.

'Perhaps you don't need him any more?' suggested Nicolas.

Did he mean because she had Herbert? Oh, she liked Herbert well enough, he was turning out to be far better than she had imagined, to have more humour as well as possibilities – by the time he was done she fancied he would have removed all traces of his mother from the bungalow – but he could never quite replace her father. No, Nicolas did not mean that.

'You don't need anyone in that way now. Life is going in all sorts of other directions for you.' Nicolas paused. He had two things to tell her, he went on, one good and one not so good. Which would she prefer to have first? Oh, the good! To give her strength to bear the bad. 'Very well.' He had talked to her mother about her music and she had agreed that Ellen should have every encouragement to pursue it. She had agreed that Ellen could come for a lesson to him every afternoon after school, on one condition; that she went home afterwards in time to have her evening meal with them. 'I think that is very reasonable, don't you?'

She thought it very reasonable also. And Herbert was going to buy her a piano! It was definitely decided. He was to take her to town the following Saturday to choose one.

'So life is not going to be so bad, eh, Ellen?'

No, she admitted, it was not, although she knew she

150

would never really feel that the bungalow was her home. She might feel more at home in it but life in the suburbs with the rows and rows of neat little houses and the dead streets and the dead people were still not, and never would be, for her.

'Maybe not all the people are dead?' said Nicolas, a twinkle in his eye.

'Not my kind, then,' she amended. She belonged in the city and that was where she would live again as soon as the choice was hers. The centre of Edinburgh or the centre of Paris. Stockbridge or the Left Bank. The Rue de la Huchette perhaps. The fishing cat street was much too narrow and lacked light for actual living. All right for hanging about in, chatting to madly eccentric and interesting characters and sniffing the night air rich with the smells of cooking and French cigarettes. She glanced across at Nick's photograph. Nicolas saw her look.

'And now for the bad news, I'm afraid.' He wasted no time. 'Nick phoned last night.'

'He's not coming?' she cried.

'I'm afraid not. He has measles. I'm sorry, Ellen.'

'It's not his fault.' It was just her luck.

'He may come later, in September.'

By September the school dance would long since be over and forgotten, would not even be a talking point. She asked politely about Nick's health and hoped he would make a quick recovery.

'I'm sorry you've been disappointed.'

'You must be disappointed too.'

'I am. But he'll come in the autumn and you could take him around then perhaps?'

'Perhaps.' He was fading already, this tall, dark and handsome boy with the smiling eyes who had walked the streets of Paris with her, drunk coffee at the boulevard cafés, talked of painting and books, leaned on the bridges of the Seine to look down at the great river. Losing people seemed easy. Would Nicolas disappear? Would she ring the bell one day and Mavis come to answer the door to tell her he did not exist, never had, and that she must have imagined him?

'Why are you staring at me like that, Ellen?'

'I was wondering . . . if you were real.'

'Come, pinch me!'

Laughing, she did, but gently, and he laughed too. Was she ready now to go back to the piano, to give her attention to that, concentrate her energies there? He sensed great energy in her body. She walked the room, between the piano and the window, the bookcases and the flowers, the fireplace and the round mahogany table on which he kept the book he was reading, his spectacles, his pen.

Not yet, she said. But she would be soon. No hurry, he declared, she must come to it when the moment was right, he would be here.

'Will you go to your dance, Ellen? I hope so. Surely all the girls will not have partners.'

They might not, but she had talked so much of Nick and bringing him that it would be a terrible anti-climax if she turned up alone. Besides, no one would ever believe he had existed at all. She could take his photograph along to prove it, suggested Nicolas. She laughed, blushed a little, but did not look at the photograph now. Nicolas did not believe that she could not find another partner for the dance. If only he were younger!

She would have to tell Isadora that Nick had been called away to Paris. On urgent business. It was all very hush-hush, to do with diplomatic circles, and Interpol might be involved. And now she must go to find Isadora and Davie for she had not seen them yesterday after promising that she would. They might be searching streets and alleys and raking in the bushes of the Botanics cursing her as they went.

Isadora was not at home. 'She's gone out with William,' said her mother. Sweet William? asked Ellen. He was quite a nice boy whatever his name was, said Mrs MacBain, Isadora had gone out with him before and she herself had liked him better than half the others that had hung around in the street eyeing their door.

Davie was sitting on the top step of his stairs, his elbows on his knees, staring into space.

'Hello,' he said. 'I thought you'd abandoned us.'

TWELVE

They sat side by side on the step. It was a long time, or seemed so, since Ellen had been inside the stair. After Herbert's street it appeared dim, felt chilly, and smelt strange. Oh, not that she had been seduced by bungalow land! There was certainly more fresh air out there, admitted Davie, but one could not live by fresh air alone. He was right, agreed Ellen solemnly. She felt as if she had come back on a pilgrimage, to visit old haunts and lay some ghosts.

'Are you there, Granny Morrison?' she called out through cupped hands, then made a ghostly sound like a banshee wailing. Davie giggled. Granny Morrison probably was there and would appear any minute and say, 'Is that you, Ellie Ferguson?' Ellen's voice came with his simultaneously: 'I might have known it!'

Their laughter echoed in the well of the stair, quite unghost-like. If Granny Morrison did appear Ellen would tell her that it was not her, merely a shade of her former self.

'Do I look like a shade?'

'Not much. Although, come to think of it, you are thinner, Ellie.'

'Honestly?'

'Honestly.'

She beamed upon him. Now that she came to think

of it she had been in the chip shop much less recently, life had been too busy one way and another, and she had done a lot of walking since moving to the South Side. It was a long pull up from Stockbridge to Princes Street, and up the Mound to the High Street.

'I don't think you've grown any either,' said Davie, speaking more cautiously this time.

He had to stand up so that they could measure. She put her hand over the top of his head and it came level with the tip of her nose. Previously he had only come up to her chin.

'Hey, I think I've shrunk!'

'I think I've grown,' said Davie diffidently.

'Fantastic! Congratulations.'

They sat down again and Davie produced a greyish bag containing liquorice allsorts. Ellen hesitated for a moment not wanting to spoil her new-found slenderness but Davie said a couple wouldn't do any harm so she succumbed. They chewed. Davie gave her a sidelong look.

'What's been happening to you?' He always knew when something had. He was a bit like Sherlock Holmes, she often said: a couple of clues and he was off on a line of deduction.

'Enough to fill a book.' One of these days she might write the story of her life − true confessions − and then all would be revealed. In the meantime, could she have another liquorice allsort, preferably an all-liquorice one?

'What *has*, Ellie?'

'They've told me the truth at last!'

'Come on, be serious. For once.'

But she was. She assumed an air of injured innocence, putting her hand into the bag at the same time. 'My dad's not dead after all.'

'*What?*' Davie almost fell off the step. She pulled him back.

'He's alive and well. In Australia. Down under, you

154

know. Where the kangaroos come from. They do, don't they? Or am I confused? Heck, am I confused!'

'What *are* you talking about?'

'I'll tell you the whole story another day. Not now. But it is true, Davie, I'm not making it up: he isn't dead. I can't go into it now as I've just had a big disappointment this afternoon.'

'About your dad?'

'No, it's Nick. He's had to go back to Paris.' She could not be bothered going into the Interpol business or diplomatic hijinks for Davie; she might for Isadora.

'Is that where he came from?'

'Sort of.'

'What kind of answer's that? Either he did or he didn't.'

'If Issie was here she'd say you had no romance in your soul.'

Well, she was not here. True, said Ellen, unless she was hiding in the stair, lurking in the darkness. She cupped her hands to her mouth again and called, 'Are you there, Isadora?' The noise echoed. There was not a sound to be heard on the stair after it died away.

Off-handedly Davie asked if Nick had gone to Paris for good. Ellen sighed: she feared so. It was awful. Why did life have to keep on changing all the time? Davie said his didn't and he was getting a bit fed up with it. They propped their chins on their elbows and sat for a while not speaking. Ellen thought of Nick strolling along the *quais* of the Seine (recovered from the measles of course) stopping to browse amongst the old books and prints. What if he didn't recover, what if he died? She almost spoke the thought aloud but stopped herself in time for to admit that Nick had measles did not fit in with her sophisticated portrayal of him. No, best to let Nick go now, into the twilight of the street of the fishing cat.

'You'll miss him.'

'Of course. And I'll have no one to go to the dance with now.'

The bottom door opened, footsteps came up the first flight of stairs, the Chisholms' door opened and someone went in. Silence descended again.

'I'll go with you if you like.'

'You, Davie? But you don't dance, except for Swan Lake.'

But they didn't go for the dancing, did they? At least, that was what Isadora said. So what about it? It seemed to be important for Ellen to go to the thing and he was willing to oblige.

'Och, Davie, I couldn't.'

'Why not?'

'Folk'd laugh. Well, I mean, with you being so much smaller.'

He turned on her fiercely. He couldn't help being small any more than she could help being tall. She looked at him with astonishment: it was seldom that Davie lost his temper. At once she said she was sorry, she knew she shouldn't have said that.

'Anyway, I have grown a bit. And my dad says boys go on growing longer than girls.'

'Is that a fact?' She brightened. Maybe she wouldn't grow any more herself. In fact Herbert had measured her last night; he had stood on a stool and taken great pains to get it exactly right and at the end of the operation had pronounced her to be exactly five feet eleven. She trusted him. Her mother she would not have done knowing that she was quite capable of taking an inch off just to please her. Herbert was one of those people that George Washington would have been proud of.

'So what do you say? Do you want to go? Let them all laugh if they want to. I don't care.'

For a moment she pondered and then her face lit up and she laughed. 'Do you know what, Davie? Neither do I! I don't care either! Isn't that fantastic?' She shouted down, 'I don't care, Granny Morrison.'

'That's settled then,' said Davie.

Ellen sobered, thinking of Nick. She eyed Davie.

Would he like her to tell him about Nick? He shrugged. It was up to her, she didn't have to if she didn't want to. But she did want to, she must.

'I've never seen him, except in a photograph.'

'You've never—?' Davie almost fell off the step again. If Ellen had any more revelations like this to make she had better save them for another day.

She told him that Nick was the nephew of Nicolas, an old man she had been helping. 'The minister asked me to, you see.' No, Davie did not see, everything was swirling in a mist of confusion and she had better begin at the beginning and tell him all about it. He listened without comment until she finished. 'Well!' he declared. He shook his head. What a girl she was! Too much imagination, that was her trouble. She pouted, did not believe that you could ever have too much, the world would be a dull place with none. Maybe so, he was ready to admit that, but what he meant was that she should be aware when she was using her imagination and when she wasn't. 'Most of the time anyway. Oh well, it doesn't matter now! I hope you haven't got anything else up your sleeve?'

She unbuttoned the sleeve of her shirt and shook it. 'Look! Nothing!'

'Thank goodness for that!'

'I don't know how you put up with me, Davie.'

'Neither do I.'

She reached out and took hold of one of his curls, kept it between finger and thumb for a second, then let it spring back to his head.

'Do you know something? I'm really quite relieved Nick's not coming. I'd have been terrified. What would I have said to him? And he'd probably have been used to chic Parisienne girls.' She stretched out her jean-clad legs covered with patches of many colours. 'Come on, let's go for a walk. I feel like some exercise.'

She jumped up, gave Davie her hand and pulled him up. They raced down the stairs. On the next landing Ellen paused outside Granny Morrison's door. As Davie opened his mouth to protest she pulled the bell, hard, and then they both flew round and round the steep stairs heading down for the dim lobby that led to the door and the street.

'My last act of childhood,' said Ellen.

'Huh!'

'Look, here comes Issie. With the Sweetest William of them all.'

'She's going to the dance with him, you know.'

Fancy that! Isadora and William were approaching, hand-in-hand. Ellen called out, 'Hi, Isadora! Hi, Sweet William!'

'Hey, have you been lost again, Ellie?' asked Isadora.

'In a manner of speaking. But I'm found again too. So the hue and cry is all over.'

Overhead a window went up, lifting their heads; Granny Morrison's head, rimmed with curlers, sailed out against the sky. 'Is that you, Ellie Ferguson?'

'It is I,' answered Ellen meekly.

'She should have known,' said Davie under his breath.

'I'll have the polis after you,' said Granny Morrison. Her window went down with a bump.

'Wonder she hasn't broken her sash cords long ago,' said Davie.

'The polis might come for you in a Black Maria,' said Isadora. 'That'd be a laugh.'

'I sure hope they do. I wouldn't want to walk. Always fancied a ride in one of those vans.

'We'll need to be going, Isadora,' said William. 'Or we'll miss the start of the picture.'

'OK, William. See you, Ellie! See you, Davie!'

'See you, Issie!'

They parted.

Ellen and Davie made for the Water of Leith. After one or two dull days the weather had turned summery again, the sky above the roofs of the higher New Town houses was blue broken with wisps of white, and the green of the leaves was tipped with golden.

An old man walked his dog on the path, two boys whom they had seen before were fishing, an empty jar beside them on the bank. The man on duty at St Bernard's well nodded as they passed, he was leaning against the outside wall to sun himself. In his sitting room Nicolas would be sitting in his chair to enjoy the sun on his face. One day — though not today — she would take Davie to meet him. They would like one another, she felt confident they would.

'What's that you're humming?'

She had not realised that she had been. It was the gooseberry tune that had been running through her head, the little song she had first made up on her father's old piano. But she no longer felt like a gooseberry.

> 'Don't call me a gooseberry
> For I'm no longer alone
> Walking one on the outside
> With the other two in.'

'You're still humming.'

'Am I? Sorry.'

Davie did not mind, he only wanted to know what it was. She'd tell him sometime, play him the tune and sing the song. He grumbled a little, although not seriously, saying there were an awful lot of things she intended to tell him one of these days.

'There's lots of time though, isn't there?'

He nodded.

'Mum said would you like to come to tea?'

He said that he would.

'Herbert's taken his mother away. So you won't have her watching you while you eat.'

Davie stopped to look at her. He grinned, shook his head. She really was an idiot! She smiled at him, wrinkling her nose. They turned back on to the path. He moved a little closer to her, their arms brushed lightly, and then he took her hand in his. They walked on.

JOAN LINGARD

If you enjoyed this book, perhaps you ought to try some more of our Joan Lingard titles. They are available in bookshops or they can be ordered directly from us. Just complete the form below and enclose the right amount of money and the books will be sent to you at home.

If you would like to order books, please send this form, and the money due to:

ARROW BOOKS, BOOKSERVICE BY POST, PO BOX 29, DOUGLAS, ISLE OF MAN, BRITISH ISLES. Please enclose a cheque or postal order made out to Arrow Books Ltd for the amount due including 30p per book for postage and packing both for orders within the UK and for overseas orders.

NAME ....

ADDRESS ....

....

Please print clearly.